MERGER

KINGS OF THE BOARDROOM
BOOK 3

NANA MALONE

COPYRIGHT

This is a work of fiction. Names, characters, places, and incidents either are the product of the author's imagination or are used fictitiously, and any resemblance to actual persons living or dead, business establishments, events, or locales, is entirely coincidental.

Merger, Book 3 in the Kings of the Boardroom Series

COPYRIGHT © 2024 by Nana Malone

All rights reserved. No part of this book may be used or reproduced in any manner whatsoever without written permission of the author except in the case of brief quotations embodied in critical articles or reviews.

PROLOGUE
ATTICUS

Numbness.

It was like all color had been bleached from the world as I sat in the white waiting room, staring at the white walls, glaring at the lifeless pastels that were meant to be soothing but were just depressing.

She could not die. I had just gotten her back.

You might not be able to do anything about it.

Fuck it, why not? She had made me a promise. One I intended to make her keep. She would *not* die on me.

There was movement at the door, and I looked up to see my brother running in. Pierce was behind him, then Gavin and Rowan.

Their expressions were bleak. Each of them was pale, sweating, and terrified.

I sat ramrod straight as I watched them, unable to move. Unable to speak. Because if I did speak, if I spent any of the energy I was using to lock everything down and focus all of my positive thoughts on Gwen and her surgery, I would break. I would shatter into a billion little pieces and wash away on the wind.

Micah came over first and clapped a hand on my shoulder, and I could feel the weight of it pressing into me, trying to convey that Gwen and I would be back together again.

Gavin stood at my other shoulder. Rowan and Micah's shoulders touched, and then Pierce closed the circle. None of them spoke, but they all stood with me, covering me, giving me their strength.

When I could finally drag in a breath, I turned my attention to Pierce. He knew what I was asking without me even having to say a word.

"He's in custody. He wasn't the shooter, but I wouldn't put it past him to have paid someone."

"So there's a chance that it was a hit?"

He shook his head. "There's always a chance, but I don't know anything for sure. Right now, I'm here for Gwen."

There was more movement at the door, and I looked over, expecting to see the doctor. Instead, it was Lakewood.

Our gazes met and held. And then we both took a long breath.

In that moment, I could let go of the fact that he had wanted my wife, the fact that he loved her.

I felt nothing other than camaraderie with him, and if he could lend his energy or prayers or any of that voodoo bullshit to making her better, I knew I'd take it. Fuck, at that point, I'd have taken wishes on the stars if he had any.

I would have taken it all and given it to her. I'd happily forfeit my life for hers if it meant she would just wake up.

Lakewood said nothing. He just came over to the circle. Pierce and Rowan made a space for him, and he stood with us.

He glanced around and finally spoke softly. "I called her family. Morgan's on the way. Clarissa too. I couldn't reach Becker."

Just hearing her father's name made me grind my teeth. I lifted my gaze to Pierce. "It couldn't have been him?"

Pierce's brow furrowed. "It wouldn't make any fucking sense. You already took care of his debts. Anyone who was after him wouldn't need to send a message."

Rowan shifted on his feet. "The other concern is Jacobson. He is willing and able, and he's pissed off enough."

"Do we have eyes on him?" I asked.

This time, it was Lance who spoke up. "Yeah. I may or may not have called in a drunk driver alert on him. The cops have him too."

My brows lifted, and I assessed Lakewood again. He did love Gwen. He had conceded defeat, but he loved her enough to take care of her, regardless.

He's a better man than you are.

He was. But he had the ability to love her from afar. I would *never* give her up. Even if she hadn't chosen me, I would have stolen her and kept her until she'd changed her mind.

Better to know thyself.

"What made you think to do that?"

Lakewood shrugged. "I figured he got the news of the wedding about the same time everyone else did, and I knew wherever he was, he was probably drinking. So I just called in his car tags. He'll be occupied for a while. And if he did this, I'm hoping he hasn't had the chance to remove any evidence yet."

I nodded at him. "Smart thinking."

He shrugged. "Whatever it takes to take care of her."

These were my men. Even Lakewood. They were willing to do anything to protect her as well.

And in that moment, knowing I was surrounded by five other men who would lay down their lives for Gwen, I finally let myself break. My shoulders sagged, and the weight of the grief crushed me where I sat.

The first tear, salty and acrid, hit my lip, and I didn't even notice it. All I could do was drop my head into my hands and weep. What would I do if I lost her?

Who would I kill?

What scorch mark would I leave on this planet if someone took her from me?

An indelible one, that was for sure. Because I was nothing without her. And she could not die and leave me. I wouldn't let her.

1
GWEN

My mouth tasted and felt like someone had peed in sawdust and then packed it into my mouth.

And someone else was playing annoying bagpipes very loudly in short staccato beats. *Beep. Beep. Beep. Beep.*

Christ, why was it so loud? And I was cold. So cold.

There *was* a heat source nearby that came and went, and each time it came close, I tried with Herculean effort to reach for it. To hold on to it. It was back now. The heat climbing up my arm. Beautiful and sweet and perfect. Just what I needed to chase away the chill.

There was a rumble. "Gwen, you can do it, baby. Come on, Ness. Show me what a strong lioness you are. Open your eyes, love."

The voice sounded far away and gravelly, low-pitched. I had to strain to hear it. "That's a good girl, Ness."

The sound reminded me of Atticus. I wanted to smile, but something was in my way. I couldn't move my face.

The warmth was there, joined by another source of warmth. Higher up. Coming from my shoulder. Oh, yes. If I could just cocoon in this, I would be so warm and happy, and I'd never have to be chilly again.

"Do it, Gwen. Open your damn eyes."

I tried to frown at that. It did sound like Atticus. Why was he always so bossy?

I tried to listen to him, to move my eyelids, but God, they were heavy. Like someone had taped them shut and then placed sand bags over them.

I tried again. And that warmth, it kept spreading. It was pulsing in my hand. What was that?

"That's it, baby. Try for me."

I managed to peel one eyelid open, but the blinding light made me cringe and shut it again, trying to back away.

"Turn off the fucking lights."

I frowned. That was Atticus. Wasn't it? Why was he so far away? I wanted him closer. Much, much closer. He would be warm. God, all I wanted to do was climb in Atticus's arms and have him hold me, and kiss me, and continue what we'd started in the limo.

Limo?

My brain tried to hold on to the fleeting thought of something that had happened in the limo.

What had happened in the limo?

Chapter 1

Suddenly, I was cold again. Freezing. I tried to reach for the warmth, but the beeps were louder now. Much louder. Faster too. *Beep, beep, beep, beep.*

I tried again to open my eyes, and this time the blinding light didn't assail me. It was a softer, more muted light, and I blinked.

A stark wintergreen gaze met mine, and my heart squeezed.

Atticus.

"Thank fuck, Ness. Hi."

I tried to use my mouth. Honestly, I did. But it was packed with... Why would someone put sawdust in my mouth? Sawdust was gross, inefficient, and disgusting. But I couldn't talk.

"Can someone get that stuff out of her mouth?"

And then I realized it wasn't sawdust. It was gauze.

Someone else came. A girl. A woman. How old was she? She couldn't be much older than Morgan. She peeled something off my lips, and I thought she was going to take my skin with it. *Ouch.*

When she pulled it out, my mouth was free.

"Atticus?" I croaked.

"Yes, baby. I'm right here. I'm right here."

My voice didn't work. It was dry and scratchy and ineffectual. I glanced around, worry settling in my veins, telling me something wasn't right.

Something beeped again, and my gaze skittered to it. It

was some kind of machine that was showing green beeps going up and down, up and down, and—

That was a monitor. And I thought the sounds were my heart rate.

I was in the hospital.

And that was when it all came crashing down. I was in the damn hospital.

What had happened? What hospital? Morgan?

No. You. You are in the hospital.

I was in the hospital. Okay. The monitor was for me. What had happened?

My scrambled brain tried to piece together what was going on and how I'd gotten here, and the confusion worried me as my mind tried to figure out what I was doing in a hospital bed.

Atticus was back, holding my hand. "There was an accident, Gwen."

I frowned. "Accident?" I remembered us being in the car. We were leaving the board meeting. Atticus had given me all his shares of Pendragon. I owned it all.

My eyes went to his as I frowned, and he stroked his thumb over my knuckles. "It's okay. *You're* okay. I've got you. Do you remember anything?"

I thought again. He gave me his shares of Pendragon, and then we'd headed home. In the limo, we'd had sex.

I started to smile at that. And then something else pricked my memory, but...

Chapter 1

It was blank. All blank. I shook my head.

He nodded. "That's okay. The doctor said that you might not remember the incident."

"Incident?" I grunted through the dryness of my mouth.

He reached for the table beside my bed and brought me a cup with a straw in it, placing it gently at my lips. I took a quick sip, the cool liquid almost too much, and it backed up as I tried to swallow. Finally, the cold splash hit my gut, making it cramp, and I winced. He put the cup back on the table and sat next to me on my bed.

"Yeah, an incident. We were getting out of the limo in front of the penthouse, and then someone..."

His voice trailed.

I waited because I didn't know why he looked so sad.

"Someone shot you."

I could only blink at him slowly as my brain tried to compute the words. "Shot me?"

"Yeah. Outside of the building. You were shot in your left shoulder. You lost a lot of blood before we were able to clear the scene and get you in the ambulance."

I started to blink rapidly then, trying to compute what he was saying. The sudden wash of fear and terror was like icy water being poured directly into my veins with the ice chips still intact.

He kept smoothing his thumb over my knuckles. "You're okay, Ness. Considering how many bullets were fired, the only one that was really bad was the one in your shoulder.

But other than that, nothing major was hit. We got really lucky."

"Someone shot me?"

He nodded slowly. "Yeah, baby. Someone shot you."

"But why?"

"That, love, is what we're going to try and figure out. But right now, you don't have to do anything except get better. *I* will make sure you get better."

I watched him. His gaze was so intense on mine. It was only then that I noticed the dark shadows under his eyes. The lines around his mouth. He was still handsome. Gorgeous. Imposing. But he looked like a shell of himself.

"How long have I been here?"

He licked his lips nervously. "A week."

I tried to sit up then, and he put his gentle hand on my shoulder. "No, don't move. You came out of the surgery, but then you weren't waking up. The doc said you might just need time to heal. Which, I think you did."

"But why would anyone shoot me?"

"Like I said, I'll figure it out. And when I do, I'm going to make them regret ever touching you. Every last one of them."

When my gaze lifted to his and I saw the grief and terror there, I knew he was serious. He wouldn't rest until he had personally made them pay.

2

ATTICUS

TOMORROW.

Gwen was coming home tomorrow. *Finally*.

Two weeks in the hospital, and she was finally coming home. I had tried to get the surgeon to hold her longer, but he said there was no reason to keep her once she'd woken up and her incisions appeared to be healing. The surgery had gone well. She would need to wear a sling for a while then do some physical therapy, but she would be fine.

As if *fine* was good enough for Gwen. If she wasn't fully thriving, I was going to fucking kill someone.

I left her at the hospital with Clarissa and Morgan for a quick visit while I met with the boys. When I marched into La Table Ronde, I saw my brother first at our usual table. When his gaze lifted to meet mine, I saw a mirror of my own face. He also looked haggard and tired. The circles under his green eyes were dark and heavy. He wasn't sleeping either.

Good. None of us were going to sleep until we found out what the fuck had gone wrong. We'd been so sure, so *certain*, that we'd done everything right, only to face fucking gunfire right outside our door.

When my eyes shifted from Micah, I saw the other lads were there. Pierce, Rowan, Gavin. And then a surprise edition... *Lakewood*.

I seriously hated him a lot less these days. Clearly, I was going soft. When I got to the table, I addressed him first. "Aren't you supposed to be in London?"

As they all stood and shook my hand, Lakewood gave me a smirk. "Well, it seems my boss left me an opening. I can set my own schedule, and I can work remotely. He didn't think about that little loophole when he sent me an ocean away."

I scowled. "Noted. Next time he shall be more clear in his directive."

Lakewood knew that right now, while Gwen needed him, I wouldn't send him anywhere. The more bodies I could have on her, the better.

I took my seat and glanced around at everyone. We were tucked in the corner of the restaurant, but we could still hear diners enjoying their lunches as if all was right in the world. As if less than two weeks ago, someone hadn't tried to take my reason for existing away from me.

Chapter 2

Micah rolled his shoulders and eyed me intently. "What's the move?"

"From the minute she leaves that hospital tomorrow, she is *never* alone. I want all of us on her so tight that you fuckers will be able to see my handprint on her ass. Do I make myself clear?"

Pierce's brows lifted. "I sent you the new security plan. The guys will be done with the penthouse and the new biometric panel today. They already finished setting it up. All you have to do is get her to pick her new passcode."

"And it's set with the biometrics?"

He nodded. "For everyone on the approved list."

We'd fucked up somewhere. We'd only had our eyes on Dad, and at the time Gwen was shot, he was in fucking custody. To our knowledge, he didn't have time to make any calls as we'd ambushed him with the marriage news. So we needed to go back to our original assumption that he was the one behind everything and figure out where the fuck we went wrong.

Pierce continued. "In the meantime, she'll have round the clock guards in a three-man rotation, one outside the building, two on the door, always."

I turned to glower at my friend. "Make it five."

Pierce lifted his brow. "Are you serious? That means taking at least one off your mother for the time being."

Was he giving me excuses? I stared him down, and he put up his hands. "Okay, I hear you. I'll make it work. I need to hire some more men. Micah, I'll need your help for background checks."

Micah nodded at him. "You've got it." He was watching me as if he wanted to say something. As if he had a judgment up his sleeve.

Rowan sat forward on his seat. "On my end, as soon as she is able and mobile, I'm going to get her started on protection training. I'll run the basics. Anti-kidnapping, self-defense, basic weaponry."

I nodded my thanks.

Lakewood shrugged. "Right, since she is just as good a hacker as I am, I have no skills to offer her other than keeping her mind off everything. Particularly, you not giving her any breathing room."

I scowled at him. "If you don't like it, you can leave."

His gaze narrowed imperceptibly, and he leaned back in his seat, an insolent smile playing on his lips. "Oh no, it's going to be fun watching your self-destruction. Has it entered your mind that maybe you should talk to her? You know Gwen is not going to want all of this."

Was he daring to tell me what my wife would want? Did he think he knew her better than I did? Did he really fucking think that he had a direct link to her heart? She wasn't going to enjoy it, but she'd understand. She would know that I needed to do this. That I needed to keep her safe. She'd get it.

"Well, the next time she's in *your* bed, you can ask her."

Chapter 2

Instantly, I realized what I had said. My own actions had shoved her into his bed just a few weeks ago.

His response was an evil grin. "You fuck this up, and she'll be right back there."

My brother placed a hand on my chest before I could launch myself over the table and punch him like I wanted to. "Lance, shut it." Micah turned to me then, his hand pressed firmly on my chest. "Lakewood is an ass. Ignore him. But... He may or may not have a point here. Look, there isn't a single one of us that wouldn't go to war with you. Whatever you need, if you ask it, we'll do it. Gwen is family."

"She's not family, you idiot. She is a queen. The crown-fucking-jewel. I almost lost her two weeks ago because *we* all got lazy. She is literally everything. If I lose her—" I worked hard to quell the shiver that traveled up my back. "So we're not losing her. *I* am not losing her. Do you understand?"

Micah nodded slowly. "I hear you, and I get it, but Lakewood's right. If you don't give that woman some breathing room, she's going to resent it. You know what happens when you decide things without talking to her."

Low blow.

"That won't be a problem anymore. She has me over a barrel. She has all my Pendragon shares. I'm just the little CEO. She'll understand that this is necessary. This is important."

My brother shrugged. "She might. Or she'll feel like a prisoner. So maybe just talk to her. Don't change her safety protocols without telling her first. You'll probably find that she agrees with half of them anyway. Want as I am to agree with anything Lakewood says, she's probably going to hate this."

"It's for her own good."

As I gave out more marching orders, I ran through some of the changes at work that would happen at Pendragon with Micah and Lakewood. I might as well put him to work if he refuses to go back to London. But part of me couldn't help but wonder if the two of them were right.

Would she understand?

She had to. She would have to see that I was only trying to keep her safe. Without her, I was nothing. I had to protect her with everything I had. I could not lose her again.

3

GWEN

ATTICUS WAS HOVERING.

Doesn't he have the right to hover?

Okay, fine. Admittedly, I'd been shot. And we still didn't know who'd done it. So there was that. But this constant watchfulness, as if I was going to shatter like glass at any moment, had to stop.

The problem was he wasn't talking to me. I tried bringing it up at the hospital yesterday, but he just told me not to worry about anything and to rest. That I could think about all these difficult things after I rested. What the hell did that mean? I had done nothing but rest and stare at the ceiling of my stupid hospital room for two weeks.

When I'd tried to use my laptop the other day, he'd just taken it out of my hands and told me that I didn't need to worry myself about any of it. If my dear husband was not careful, I was going to whack him on the head with said laptop.

The worse part was when I told him my nefarious plan to whack him over the head. Instead of calling me a violent little thing like he normally would have, he just kissed me on the forehead and patted my hand. Like I was a child who didn't know what I was saying.

Well, *he* would certainly know what I was saying when I actually did it. Now all I needed to do was find out where he'd *hidden* the laptop.

Our door staff at the penthouse was discreet. All Manny did was give me a soft smile and say, "Welcome back, Mrs. Price."

I considered it for a moment. I hadn't even really had the opportunity to *enjoy* being called Mrs. Price. We'd been hiding our marital status when we got back from the Winston Isles. We'd only announced it the day I got shot.

I'd never been that girl who wanted to change my name and do all the bride things, but there was something nice about saying that I belonged to someone and he belonged to me.

Though before I filed any paperwork, I needed to make sure I wasn't going to super-hyphenate my name. Gwenyth Christin-Becker-Price. That was too much. I didn't want to completely lose myself just because I was married to one of the world's most powerful men.

But you are one of the world's most powerful women now.

Chapter 3

You hold a tech conglomerate in your hands. You have all the shares.

Shit.

That was right. All of Atticus's Pendragon shares were now mine. Just thinking about the sheer number of them made me feel powerful as hell. But maybe, just maybe, I might be able to use some of that as leverage to get my husband to back the fuck off.

"Are you okay? Are you tired? Do you want me to carry you?"

We stepped in the elevator, and I slid him a withering glare. "If you pick me up, I swear before God that only one of us will be walking into the penthouse in a few minutes. And despite what you think, it will not be you."

He pressed his lips together. Gone was the humor that would have lightened the mood. There was no teasing like before when he would have said, "We'll see about that," or something else that made me giggle.

"You know I'll be okay, right?" I asked.

"Of course, you just need to heal up."

I glowered down at my sling. "I don't have to wear this thing all the time. The surgery scar is healing well. And honestly, you and I both know that I'm fine. The bullet didn't hit anything vital. The only thing that was scary was the blood loss and possibility of sepsis. And that's already taken care of. Please chill out, okay?"

He didn't say anything. And I was surprised when we reached our floor and there was another door.

"What the hell is this?"

"Additional security. Give me your palm."

I lifted my brow. I was so shocked I couldn't move as Atticus took my left hand, planted it on the panel, and typed in a few things to lock it in. "Now you're approved. Only you. Anyone else will have to get buzzed up and ring the doorbell."

I blinked slowly. "Well, it's not like they can access the penthouse elevator without a key anyway."

He shrugged. "Just in case."

When we stepped in the foyer, we were greeted by the scent of spices and food cooking, and I swear to God I would have kissed Magda on the mouth if she'd been standing right there.

"Oh my God. Is that bread? I would kill for fresh-baked bread. Wow, this is great."

His smile was brief as he nodded toward what looked like a new security panel.

"This is the new panel?" I asked.

"There's a new manual too. You will need to read it."

"Why do we need a new security panel? Wasn't the other one state of the art?"

"Yes, but this one is better. Come here. If you put your chin right there and—" He cut himself off as he pressed a couple of buttons on the side and indicated that I should put

Chapter 3

my chin in the little tray and look directly at the light. "Perfect. Now we have your handprint, fingerprint, and eye scan. And you see the monitor here? You'll be able to see who's downstairs in the lobby and know who's in the stairwells."

He flicked through the images quickly, showing me. "And you'll also be able to see anyone from the panic room."

I blinked at him slowly. "Uh, there's a panic room now? I have only been gone two weeks, or did you put this in while we were in the Winston Isles?"

"If you pay enough money and tell them that they don't have to be concerned about any noise complaints, anything can be done in two weeks."

Looking on the monitor, I took in the size of the panic room. "That's a whole full-sized room."

He nodded. "Well, I took part of the study, part of the library, and that fifth bathroom. We didn't need it."

I stared at him in disbelief. "You took part of the library?"

"Yes. It made the most sense for the space."

My heart squeezed. This didn't feel like *my* Atticus. This was cold, calculated Atticus. The one who would do the important thing, but not necessarily the one that would make anyone happy.

"I'm really grateful, Atticus. I am. And I love that you love me enough to do all of this for me. I appreciate it. I really do."

His back went ramrod straight. "Yes, *but?*"

I winced. "No but. It's just... You and Micah and I all loved that library. It's just a shame to see some of that go."

"Don't worry. I'll buy you a library if that's what you want." Then he marched from the foyer, leaving me and taking my bags with him. I had no choice but to follow. But something was off. Where was the Atticus who had been laughing with me, holding me, and making me comfortable? Where had he gone?

When I rounded the corner, I heard voices and gasped in surprise as I saw Clarissa and Morgan on the couch. "Oh my gosh, what are you guys doing here?"

Morgan jumped up and bounded over to me, but Atticus stopped her right before she reached me, and he frowned. "You have to be careful with her, Morgan. You can't jostle her too much, remember?"

Morgan winced in contrition. "Fuck, I'm so sorry. It's just so great to see you walking around instead of lying down. You look so good."

"You're a liar," I teased. "But I am happy to be home."

Atticus was watching me and apparently felt the need to chime in. "You're always beautiful, Gwen."

"Yes, well, you're my husband. You are legally obligated to say that."

Again, no real smile. Not even the ghost of one that I was more familiar with.

Clarissa came over and hugged me gently. "Morgan and I have been baking since we saw you in the hospital a couple of days ago. There is bread galore. I know that's what you like to eat when you're feeling sad, so there are some baguettes and a few croissants for you. We just wanted to see you. I know that you and Atticus probably want to get reacquainted with your home."

Morgan whined. "But I don't want to leave. I want to use the sauna."

Atticus nodded at her. "Of course, you can use it."

Clarissa shook her head. "We appreciate it, but we're going. Come on, Morgan. We just wanted to see that your sister got home okay."

I took both their hands. "We didn't even get to visit."

Clarissa set her gaze over at Atticus and shook her head. "Something tells me that the two of you need a little alone time, okay? We'll come see you later this week. We will do Friday dinner here instead of at the house."

Atticus interjected, "Yes, that's better. I wouldn't have let her come to the house."

Again, not kidding. He was deadly serious. What was wrong with him? And who the hell had replaced my husband with a robot? I got that maybe he was scared for me, or worried. But this was something different. This wasn't him. And if he kept this behavior up, we were going to have a real problem on our hands.

4

GWEN

When Clarissa and Morgan were gone, Atticus seemed to relax slightly. The frigid temperature of his soul warmed up by several degrees. But it seemed to stop and hover much lower than normal, never fully warming to a blast furnace like I was used to. He insisted that I be seated in the living room on the couch, and he brought me a tray. There was soup on it, and bread, and my favorite ginger beer. "Well, now you're just spoiling me."

"You *should* be spoiled."

"Where's Magda? I expected her to be here, mother-henning me."

He frowned. "You don't need Magda to mother-hen you. I'm perfectly capable."

I shrugged. "Okay, I'm just making conversation. What is wrong with you? You're acting weird."

Chapter 4

"I'm not acting weird. This is me, a man who had to watch his wife get shot two weeks ago. And now she's home and insisting on working and doing things for herself. So you can understand how I'm not feeling like myself, right?"

I sighed. "Baby, I'm okay. I didn't mean to scare you."

The lines on his brow only deepened. "*You* didn't mean to? It wasn't your fault, Gwen. It was mine. We were so busy trying to prove what my father had done that we didn't see how dangerous he really was, or we didn't see the fact that there was another danger entirely. That's on me. We didn't even look for another suspect. We just narrowed in, and I almost got you killed. I—"

For the first time in two weeks, I saw him break again, finally allowing himself to be vulnerable with me. I tried to adjust the tray with one arm, and he quickly moved it to the coffee table for me. "What do you need, Gwen?"

"I need this." Awkwardly, I climbed into his lap and tucked myself in, burrowing my face into his chest. I inhaled deeply, letting his scent wrap around me and warm me up even more as I nuzzled in.

"Atticus, I can't even imagine what you went through, knowing I'd been hurt. And I can see how that would make you wary."

"I'm not wary, Gwen. I'm incensed. Because I fucked up. My wife almost died."

"Excuse me, Mr. Price, but I think there is enough blame to go around. We *all* were looking elsewhere. And for all we know, your father hired someone to do the shooting. So before we go jumping to conclusions and all that, let's think for a minute, okay?"

"Think? What do you think I've been doing for two weeks? I'm trying to figure out how to wrap you in a bubble and how to get him to confess what he knows. Trying to make it safe for you. I've *been* thinking."

I could tell he couldn't understand me right now. He was still too wrapped up in his grief. "Okay, I hear you. Why don't we go to bed?"

He nodded and helped me up. Earlier, he'd put my bags in our room. I hadn't even stepped foot in there yet. I quickly got ready for bed with some assistance. I would be glad when I no longer needed his help for that. But the maneuvering of my bra one handed was still not quite manageable. Maybe I would just go braless from now on.

You still have to go to the office, so you'd better not.

Yeah. Not the brightest idea.

When I climbed into bed, Atticus helped me onto my side. "Why aren't you ready for bed yet?" I asked when I noticed he hadn't undressed.

"I have some things that I need to look over in the study. But I'll be close by if you need me. I'd work in here, but it feels creepy to watch you sleep."

"Don't you watch me sleep anyway?"

And there it was, his little hidden smile. The one he saved for me. Why had it taken so long to find him?

Chapter 4

When he tucked me in, he leaned in close, and I tilted my lips up for a kiss. But instead, his hands planted on my cheeks ever so gently and guided my head down so he could kiss my forehead.

What the hell?

"Atticus? What, you're not kissing me now?"

His gaze shifted to my lips. "I did kiss you."

I considered him for a long moment. "Actually, no, you didn't. And you haven't. Not since I've been home. We've been here for hours, and not once have you pressed your lips to mine."

He frowned. "Of course I have."

Bullshit. "Don't you gaslight me. You haven't. And what the hell is up?"

He frowned. "Nothing is up. You want a kiss? Here's a kiss." He leaned in, his body rigid, as if I was going to accept that as a kiss. I turned my head. "No. Where's my *real* kiss? You know, the one where you missed me and only had your hand for companionship for the last couple of weeks? I feel like we were supposed to get started on christening the whole house. What happened to that?"

He stared at me like I'd lost my head and replaced it with two strange ones. "Are you insane? You're hurt."

He had to be kidding. "Yes, my shoulder *is* hurt. But I am horny. Why aren't you doing something about that?"

He pressed his lips together firmly. "We can't. Not until you've healed up. The way I want you—"

There he was. In that moment, I could see the Atticus I was used to. The one who was obsessed with me. The one who, at any given moment, would drop to his knees, just for the pleasure of eating me. The one who fucked me so good in the back of the car that I'd seen stars. He was in there, so why wasn't he coming out to play?

"What's going on?" I asked. "I know you want me. I can see it. It's right there."

He swallowed hard and looked away. "That's no secret. I always want you. Right now, I need to do what's *best* for you, which is for you to get some sleep. I'll check on you before I go to bed."

Frustrated and well... horny, I eased back on my satin pillowcase. I couldn't believe it. "Fine, I guess, but—" It took me a moment to filter through what he'd said. He would look in on me. Which meant he wasn't planning on sleeping here. "Where the hell are you going to be sleeping?"

"Next door."

I blinked at him. And then I slowed down that blink, so he would get the point. "That's pure insanity. Why?"

"Jesus, Gwen, why are you being like this? This is for *you*. You'll get better rest without me here. You won't be tempted to starfish and roll around onto your shoulder. This is for the best."

"Who decided that though? And hello, your wife just said she is horny. The husband I know would have immedi-

Chapter 4

ately dropped to his knees, bent my legs into a pretzel, and eaten me for an hour. What is going on?"

His gaze flickered to my lips again. "So let me get this straight; you want me to *service* you?"

That fun playful part of me inside prickled slightly. Why was he being like this? "No, I'm not demanding that you *service* me. I just want to be with my husband. You know, the man I married. The man who loves me, and I love him."

"I'm just trying to do right by you. And right now, that means giving you space and time to heal before... How did you say it? Before I bend you like a pretzel." He pushed to his feet.

"So, is that like *ever* coming back on the table? The whole pretzel thing?"

He didn't bother to answer me. Instead, he quietly walked out of our room to go and sleep somewhere else.

5
ATTICUS

"Fucking take it. *You are such a good wife, taking my big cock all the way down your throat.*"

I wound my fingers into my wife's hair and tugged savagely, angling her head to take my cock all the way down and hit the back of her throat. When it did, she lifted her eyes. Her glittering gaze met mine and my control snapped as I started to fuck to her face. She took it, moaning around the length of my—"

"Atticus, oh my God, Atticus."

Gwen's wrenching scream jolted me out of bed, and I growled when I shoved the sheets off and saw the state of my cock.

It didn't deter me that my dick was still raging. I ran quickly toward her room and shoved open the door to find her thrashing in bed. I ran to the side of the bed and placed

Chapter 5

my hand on her good shoulder gently. "Gwen, baby. Open your eyes. It's me. It's me, Atticus. Open your eyes. You're safe. I'm here. I'm here, baby. I'm here."

When her eyes cracked open, she gasped, dragging in air raggedly through her lungs. "Oh my God. Oh my God."

I checked her sling first. It was still in place. "You're okay, baby. What is it? Did you hit your shoulder? Are you in pain?"

She frowned as if getting her bearings, trying to figure out what was going on herself. "I-I dreamed you weren't... I needed you, and you weren't there. I don't... I don't know."

My heart that had been galloping out of my chest started to steady once again. "It was just a dream. I'm always here when you need me. See, I'm right here."

I lifted her good arm and placed her hand on my chest. "See? I'm right here. I'm right where you need me."

"I was so scared. You weren't here, and I needed you, and—"

I tugged her close, lifting her gently and being careful of her shoulder. "I'm sorry, babe. I'm here. See?"

Gwen fisted her hand in my T-shirt. "Please don't leave me. Can you hold me for a while?"

Hold her? In bed? After the dream I had just woken up from? My cock throbbed in my pajama bottoms. With her, I didn't need to wear them. At least we'd gotten over that habit. But I'd taken to wearing them again, just in case.

"That's not a good idea, Ness. But look, I'll be right here until you go back to sleep."

She whined. "I'm telling you I need you, and you're telling me not right now. What is going on, Atticus?"

She drew her hand down over my chest, and I swear before God, I could not have held back the shudder that racked through my body in that moment.

"Don't you want me anymore? Did me getting shot change something?"

"Of course not," I groaned. "I'll always want you."

Her hand spread out all over my chest and down my abdomen. Just as she was about to wrap her hand around my cock, I stopped her with my other hand. "Uh, that's not a good idea."

"What are you talking about, Atticus? You're hard. You're very, very hard. I can see for myself. Why won't you let me touch you?"

Fuck, this was torture. I was not strong enough to hold out. This had been a bad idea. I should have taken her back to her old apartment. Or anywhere I didn't have to sleep next to her, trying not to touch her. That had never been anything I even considered.

"Gwen, be reasonable. I'm here. But until you're healed up, this is not what we're doing. I don't want to risk hurting you. It would kill me, darling. Do you understand?"

"No, I don't understand. You're pushing me away, and I don't know what to do."

Chapter 5

"Gwen," I muttered through clenched teeth. Christ, all I wanted to do was hold her. All I wanted was her in my arms. But if I did, I could lose control, hurt her in my sleep. And fuck me, if I touched her how I wanted to, how she was asking me to...

No. That wasn't what she needed right now. She needed rest and tenderness. Not the dicking down she *thought* she wanted. I wasn't great at being tender, but I could at least take care of her. Show her that I *deserved* to take care of her... even though I'd fucked up. I had to keep myself out of her bed, or I was going to ruin everything.

But she didn't see it my way. "So, you're not going to even touch me?"

I shook my head. "No. I'm not. You need to get a clean bill of health before we resume any physical activities."

Her gaze slid over me and straight down to my cock. Asshole soldier that he was, he saluted her. Because he didn't give two fucks about her shoulder. He hadn't been scared half to death. Only that he had to be stuck with me for the rest of his miserable life.

"Are you sure this isn't... Have your feelings— changed?"

I stared at her for a long moment. What the fuck did she mean? The answer was in the way she bit her bottom lip. The uncertainty in her gaze. Oh, for fuck's sake. She thought I didn't want her?

I planted both hands on her cheeks. "Gwen, I don't think you understand the depths to which I want you. If you *did* understand, you would probably run for your life. You are *everything*. You always have been. So, let's go ahead and pretend you didn't say some utterly insane shit and get you back to sleep so you can heal."

She seemed to buy it. Nodding against my hold. This time, I gave in a little bit and planted a soft kiss on her lips. And the electric spark of need tried to claw its way out of my chest.

And that is why we don't kiss the wife we crave. Because this shit is not what she needs.

Fucking hell. I had to force myself to pull back. "This has nothing to do with not wanting you. I'm trying to keep you safe."

"Were you going to ask if I *want* to be kept safe from you, or were you just going to decide?"

I shrugged. "Sometimes we don't know what's good for us. I think this might be one of those cases."

I sat with her until she fell asleep again, all the while thinking of all the ways I could calm down my raging dick. I'd been without her for two weeks. I had bargained with every god I could think of just to let her live.

I'd made a million deals with the devil just to keep her safe. And now, she wanted to tempt fate? There was absolutely no way I was doing that. If I touched her, I wouldn't have the control I needed, and that would hurt her more. The way I saw it, I had already done enough damage.

6

ATTICUS

I SAT on the edge of the bed, staring at Gwen as she fumbled with a bottle of nail polish. Her arm was wrapped in her sling, and she was trying to balance the tiny brush between her fingers, but it was clear she was struggling. I watched her for a moment longer, torn between stepping in to help and giving her the space she seemed to crave. Finally, I cleared my throat.

"What are you doing?" My voice came out rougher than I intended, but I couldn't help it. Every time I looked at her, all I could see was the moment she got shot, the blood, the panic.

Gwen glanced up at me and smiled, though I could tell it was forced. "I'm trying to paint my toenails," she said sweetly, like it was the most normal thing in the world. "I thought it might help me feel a bit more like myself."

The pang of guilt ripped through me. She was trying so hard to hold onto some semblance of normalcy, and here I was, hovering over her like a goddamn helicopter. I had been doing that a lot lately. Hovering, watching, waiting for something else to go wrong. I wanted to say something reassuring, but all I could think about was how close I came to losing her.

"We can call someone to do that for you," I offered, my tone more practical than comforting. It was an easy solution. Hire someone. Delegate the task. Keep her safe. But Gwen just shook her head, her smile fading slightly.

"With the security concerns, I assumed you didn't trust anyone," she said quietly.

Fuck.

She was right. I didn't trust anyone. Not after what happened. I was paranoid, constantly on edge, and it was affecting her too. I didn't want to admit it, but the fear that gnawed at my insides was consuming me. It was making me question everything and everyone. And it was pushing Gwen away.

I swallowed hard and nodded. "You're right. I don't trust anyone."

She sighed and went back to her task, her fingers trembling slightly as she tried to unscrew the cap with one hand. I watched her struggle for a few more seconds before the tension became too much. I couldn't stand it anymore.

"I'll do it," I said abruptly.

Chapter 6

Gwen looked up at me, surprise flickering in her eyes. "What?"

"I'll paint your toenails," I repeated, my voice firm. It was the least I could do. I owed her that much.

She blinked at me, clearly taken aback. "You don't have to—"

"I want to," I interrupted. "Please, let me do this."

She hesitated for a moment, then nodded, a small smile tugging at the corners of her lips. "Okay," she said softly.

I took the nail polish from her hand and knelt down in front of her, gently lifting her foot onto my lap. My hands shook as I unscrewed the cap and dipped the brush into the polish. I couldn't remember the last time I did something so delicate, so intimate. I was used to handling contracts, weapons, making deals that could change the course of nations. But this? This was different. This was personal.

I carefully applied the polish to her toenails, concentrating on each stroke, making sure the coverage was even, that I didn't miss a spot. The silence between us was heavy, but not uncomfortable. It was as if the act itself spoke volumes, more than any words could.

As I worked, I could feel the emotions bubbling up inside me, emotions I had been trying to suppress since the day she got shot. Guilt, fear, anger at myself for letting it happen, for not protecting her the way I should have. I blamed myself for everything. If I had been more vigilant, more cautious, maybe she wouldn't have gotten hurt.

I heard her sigh softly, and when I looked up, her eyes were on me, filled with a mixture of affection and concern. "Atticus," she began, her voice tender.

I shook my head, cutting her off. "Don't, Gwen. Don't try to make this better. I should have protected you. I should have seen the threat coming. I should have—"

"Atticus," she said again, more firmly this time. "It wasn't your fault."

I clenched my jaw, the brush in my hand stilling as I fought to keep my emotions in check. I wanted to believe her, but the guilt was too overwhelming, too consuming. "It was," I muttered. "I let my guard down. I failed you."

Gwen reached out with her good hand, gently cupping my cheek, her touch warm and reassuring. "You didn't fail me," she insisted. "You did everything you could. And I'm still here, because of you."

I closed my eyes, leaning into her touch, trying to absorb the comfort she was offering. But it was hard. Too hard. I was supposed to be the strong one, the protector, the one who kept her safe. But I had failed, and the weight of that failure was crushing me.

I finished painting her toenails in silence, each stroke of the brush a reminder of how close I came to losing her. When I was done, I gently blew on her toes to help the polish dry, my heart heavy with the words I couldn't say. The words that were lodged in my throat, choking me.

"I love you," Gwen whispered, her voice barely audible.

I looked up at her, my chest tightening. I wanted to say it back, to tell her how much she meant to me, how terrified I was of losing her. But the words wouldn't come. They were stuck, buried under layers of guilt and self-recrimination.

Instead, I nodded, the corners of my mouth lifting in a small, sad smile. "I love you too," I said, my voice rough and unsteady.

Gwen smiled, a tear slipping down her cheek as she leaned forward and kissed me, her lips soft and warm against mine. The kiss was brief, but it was enough to remind me of what I almost lost, of what I needed to protect at all costs.

When she pulled back, she wiped her tear away with the back of her hand and chuckled softly. "You did a pretty good job," she said, wiggling her toes. "I might have to hire you as my personal pedicurist."

I let out a shaky laugh, grateful for the brief moment of levity. "I'll add it to my resume," I joked, though my heart wasn't really in it.

Gwen watched me for a moment, her expression softening as she reached out and took my hand in hers. "Atticus," she said gently, "you don't have to carry this burden alone. We're in this together."

I squeezed her hand, the warmth of her touch grounding me, anchoring me in the present. "I know," I murmured, though the guilt still lingered, a shadow that refused to dissipate.

She smiled at me, that sweet, genuine smile that made

my heart ache. "We'll get through this," she said with quiet conviction. "Together."

I nodded, though I wasn't sure I believed her. But for her sake, I would try. I would do whatever it took to keep her safe, to make sure she never had to go through something like this again.

As I helped her back onto the bed and tucked her in, I leaned down and kissed her forehead, the simple act bringing a lump to my throat. "Get some rest," I whispered, my voice thick with emotion.

Gwen looked up at me, her eyes filled with love and trust, and for a moment, I felt a glimmer of hope. Maybe, just maybe, we could get through this. Together.

As I turned off the light and left the room, I made a silent vow. I would protect her, no matter what. I would keep her safe, even if it meant pushing her away, even if it meant sacrificing my own peace of mind. Because she was worth it. She was everything.

And I couldn't bear the thought of losing her again.

7

GWEN

A FEW MORE DAYS AT home and Atticus finally decided to let me go into the office. I was so excited I even packed my lunch the night before.

He still refused to sleep with me, which was beyond annoying. He would kiss me goodnight at my door like I was some kind of villain trying to steal his virtue.

But at night, I could hear him in the shower, groaning my name as he came. I knew that's what he was doing. I'd tried to communicate to him that I was feeling better every day, that he didn't need to treat me like glass.

Hell, we'd had the kind of sex that was probably banned in several countries. It wasn't even the sex I missed most, though I did miss that. But even more, I missed the way he would look at me, the questions he would ask, trying to probe at a deeper level. Now he just looked at me like I was on a pedestal, like I was someone to protect. Something to own. Something to take down and polish every once in a while then put back. Not like I was the woman he loved. But we were going to deal with that. It had been a rough few weeks, and we just needed to get into our groove again. I started physical therapy in a few days, and hopefully, once he saw that I wasn't going to shatter and break at the slightest provocation, he would relax just a little and let me breathe. Because we could not sustain the way things were right now. I would kill him.

As I left the penthouse, I was surrounded by men. One or two I understood. But five? I had expected one of the guys I knew, and occasionally Sven or Rowan made the cut, but they were mostly guys I didn't know.

I had tried to get to know them better by chatting them up, but Atticus had made it pretty clear they were not meant to be my friends. They were meant to protect and to watch my back.

I mean, if people were watching my back, shouldn't I *like* them? So despite his growling doom and gloom mood, I was at the very least polite and welcoming. I liked to know the people I worked with.

It didn't matter though. Nothing could dampen my mood today. Back to work at last. I knew Atticus had delayed our latest release when I was in the hospital, but I needed to check on it. I also needed to have several meetings with my team, reconnect with VPs on the technology side, and make

Chapter 7

sure everything was still on track for our goals. Then I needed to find someone to explain to me exactly what I was supposed to do with all the damn shares I owned of Pendragon Tech.

I'd tried to broach the subject with Atticus a couple of days ago, but he hadn't wanted to talk about it and told me not to worry about that right now. If I could sneak some time in his calendar, I'd talk to Micah. He would know.

Morgan and my stepmother would probably say I was a workaholic. I understood why they would say that because there were times that it felt like everything I did was about the office. But I *loved* my work.

The bureaucracy aside, I loved the routine of going to the office and having people you got coffee with. Of getting the latest gossip and finding out who was dating whom. I loved my team. Every single one of them had been hand-picked by me. And it was time I got to really know the Pendragon employees too. At least the ones on this side of the ocean.

When we reached the office, it was so bizarre having to get on an elevator with five grown men. And the way they surrounded me, like the points of a star, was ridiculous. I was conspicuous, and it felt like overkill.

When we reached my floor, the one in front, Blaine, I think his name was, stepped aside to let me through. And I marched down the hall, trying to shake them a little because

I didn't want my team seeing me flanked like I was some kind of royalty or something.

But the oddest thing happened. There was someone in my office, making me hesitate when I entered. The name placard still bore my name, but a blond white guy with a ruddy face was sitting there.

"Hi, can I help you?" I asked hesitantly.

He glanced up, his wide, pale face expressive. "Oh, you're Gwen."

"That I am. The name is on the door."

"Sorry." He pushed to his feet. "I'm Jack. Atticus assigned me two weeks ago to kind of help the team keep going during your absence, and obviously, with your new responsibilities, we will be looking to transition them to me soon anyway. So I figured while the project was paused, it would be a good time to, you know, get to know everyone. Sorry for commandeering your office. I figured you'd be moving up to the suites anyway. I mean, that's if you're even going to be in the office much."

The more he talked, the more I frowned. His gaze skittered to the broody behemoth behind me, and his eyes went wide. "Oh, uh... Do you need your office now? Because I can use a cubicle until you're done."

"Done?" What the hell? I was back for good.

"Yeah. I figured you needed to pick something up. Isn't that why you're here?"

"No. I'm here to work."

Chapter 7

He blinked at me slowly. "Oh, right. I didn't know you'd be coming in to work today."

"That's strange because Atticus sure did." I stated matter-of-factly.

"Right. Okay, so like is there something in particular that you want me to do? I mean, I figured you have your hands full and the project is on hold anyway."

I narrowed my gaze at him. "Just for the record, that's *my* team out there." I was back now. Why was he under the impression that he was taking over my team?

"Oh, so no one has communicated that to you yet. Okay, well, think of me as, um, the new you. Right? I got this. Everyone seems cool, and we get on like a house on fire. So, if there's anything you need, I can tell them."

"Are you suggesting that I need an intermediary to speak to my people?"

His brows skipped up and down as if he couldn't quite see where he'd gone wrong. "Well, you know, it's probably easier that way. I mean, there's a lot of meetings and executive stuff you'll be dealing with."

"How about this, Jack; it's best *not* to assume. If I need you, I'm capable of communicating effectively. I'm trying to get my team back on track."

"Don't you worry about it," he said with a casual wave of his hand. "I've already got them under control. I'm sure Mr. Price will communicate a new release date, and then—"

"Mr. Price will *not*, in fact, communicate a new release

date," I said, my voice rising. "You're talking about *my* team, and *I* will provide a new release date."

His brows did that thing again. What the fuck was going on here? And who was this idiot, thinking that this was his team?

A saner voice prevailed in my head and told me to walk away.

I found Macy in her cubicle, and when I stepped around the corner, she grinned. "Oh, my God. You're back from the dead. Literally, I hear." She stood up and gave me a firm but gentle hug as if trying to be careful with me. "Boy, are you a sight for sore eyes."

"Who the fuck is that in my office?"

Macy rolled her eyes. "Oh, that dipshit. So friendly, that Jack, but dumber than a box of rocks. He has no idea how any of the software works. At least two or three times a day, he asks one of us, 'Oh, it doesn't do this?'." She rolled her eyes. "Where did Atticus scrounge him up from? All I know is that he showed up two weeks ago and said he's taking over the project."

She had to be kidding. "Taking over? What the hell?"

"Yeah. Something about you having new responsibilities now?"

I ground my teeth. "I do *not* have new responsibilities."

She grinned at me. "Okay... But aren't you the majority shareholder now? Like, you're the big lady boss."

Chapter 7

I glanced around, smiling at my people. They all returned shy smiles but kept on moving. Matter of fact, the activity in the bullpen, where most of the cubicles were located, was subdued. Everybody was head down and working on something, kind of like when you knew the big boss was in town and everyone made it a point to look busy because they didn't want to be the one who was slacking off, gossiping about the latest royal scandal or which celebrity was caught shagging whom.

I glanced around again. Everyone was tapping away frantically at their keyboards. This was not my team. While we worked hard and got our shit done, this tenseness wasn't the norm. What had happened to my people?

Macy could feel my unease. "Oh, don't be mad at them. They just don't know how to act. I mean, there's been a huge coup. And then everyone finds out that you married him. Because I mean, while I knew that you thought the man was hot, I didn't think you were going to *marry* him, and I'm closer to you than most of them are. And then you got shot, and now you're back, and Atticus was very clear that we were to treat you with the respect that you deserve, so it's... weird."

I stared at her. "Atticus spoke to you guys?"

"Yeah. He said that when you came back, we were supposed to treat you with utmost respect. No bullshit, because you have the company in your hands."

I scowled. "I am going to kill that man."

But as it turned out, I was going to have to wait to kill my husband. He was in back-to-back meetings all day.

I was happy to find out that he had a new assistant, Andrew. I was thrilled to learn Leah was gone, but Andrew was quite the stickler about my husband's schedule. When he saw me, his eyes went wide and he stood up immediately. "Mrs. Price."

"No, don't call me that. Call me Gwen."

He frowned. "Um, yes, Mrs. Price, Gwen. I shall try. Although, Mr. Price has indicated that you should only be called Mrs. Price."

"Well, it's me and my name, so shouldn't the way I like to be referred to take precedence?"

He rocked back and forth on his feet. "Yes, sure. Gwen."

"Do you know where my husband is?"

"Actually, he's off site at a meeting. But he did say if you ever came by or needed to see him I was to make room for you. We have an opening at about four thirty if you'd like to have that slot. He has a call scheduled at a quarter to five, sales projections for an app manufacturer, but I could squeeze you in right before that."

"Four thirty? It's ten o'clock. That's all he's got?"

"Yes, ma'am. That's all he's got right now."

Damn. "Fine. I guess I will take four thirty."

By the time lunch rolled around, I was in need of a drink.

Chapter 7

I wasn't allowed to do anything. Nothing at all. My team had been taken over by a group of Stepford Wives.

Jack was a little *too* helpful. And I couldn't get a hold of Micah. So I ended up calling my sister and Lance for lunch at Bryant Park Grill. Maybe Lance had an idea what the fuck was going on in the office. Although, he was supposed to be in London, wasn't he?

Morgan got there first. She waved when she saw me. "You look good. Even better than when I saw you a couple of days ago. A little respite at home, and probably some sexing-up from your man, has got you looking good."

I frowned. "Um, respite, yes. No sexing-up from the man yet."

Morgan lifted her brows. "You mean the very same man who usually looks like he wants to eat you? Say it isn't so."

I rolled my eyes. "We're not going to talk about it. Where's Lance?"

Morgan was in the midst of shrugging right as Lance walked through the door.

"I was going to say I hope he doesn't come. But there he is, just because you called," she muttered.

"Oh my God, can you two not bicker today? I just... I need some normalcy."

My sister just shrugged. "Lance and I bickering *is* normalcy."

She had a solid point there.

Lance gave me double kisses.

"You can't be European already," I said with a light smack to his shoulder. "You were only there for three months."

"I can be anything I want to. And you look great."

Morgan rolled her eyes and slapped down her menu. "I already told her she looked great. She doesn't need you to reiterate."

Lance opened his mouth to start in on her, and I slapped my hand on the table. "Both of you, shut it."

The waiter came over with our drink orders. Morgan just stared at me when my drink arrived and I downed half of it. "Wow. Rough day?" she asked.

"Yeah, you could say that. It's like I don't work there anymore."

Lance sat back. "What? At Pendragon? What do you mean?"

"There's this guy, Jack, and he's taken over my job." I spent the next fifteen minutes telling them about how my morning had gone. How I'd been stalled at every step and was unable to do the things I needed to do. They listened dutifully because that's what they were there for.

Lance rubbed the back of his neck. "There's no reason why you can't manage your team. It doesn't make any sense."

"Yeah, tell *him* that."

"Also, it doesn't make sense that he would put someone like Jack Farlow in that position. The guy is an idiot," Lance

Chapter 7

said, confirming Macy's earlier assessment. "The team won't respect him."

"*Again*, tell him that."

Morgan piped up. "Have you talked to Atticus about it?"

"No, he was at an off-site meeting. And as you see, I have my bodyguards out there." Two of them, Sven and some other guy, were at a table near us. The others were at the exits. "And then I was left to fend for myself but without any information. Lance, you must know something."

Lance shook his head. "No, nothing that would impede your work. But..."

He snapped his mouth shut then and shook his head.

I knew Lance. He was keeping something quiet. "What's up? Spill it."

"No, it's just... Atticus said something the other day, that you were 'the crown jewel and we had to protect you at all cost.'"

What the hell did that mean? I wasn't some asset to protect. I was his wife. "But how is not letting me work protecting me? That's ridiculous. Besides, I think he fell in love with my brain first, so it really makes no sense."

Lance shrugged. "He did also say that you might have to be protected from yourself as well."

I lifted my brows. "He said what?"

Lance winced. "You know he's not my favorite person. However, up until two weeks ago, he was *your* favorite person, so that's on you. But I think he's just really freaked out and worried about you."

This was insane. He was talking to Lance before he was talking to me? "He won't even have sex with me."

Morgan's jaw unhinged, and Lance choked on his water before saying, "Eww. Do I need to hear this?"

Morgan shook her head. "It's okay, Lance. People have sex. You'll learn about it one day too."

He looked like he wanted to put his hands around her neck and squeeze. I put a hand on his shoulder. "Don't, okay? I don't want to get kicked out before I eat my burger."

He sighed, and Morgan did this little side-to-side jig in her seat like she was kicking her feet joyously under the table. She lived to irritate him. There was something very wrong with the two of them.

"Anyway, so he thinks he needs to protect me from myself?"

Lance winced. "I know. When you say it out loud like that, it sounds far worse than when he said it. I'm just saying that he is very much concerned about your wellbeing."

"Concerned, is he? In that case, I think my husband and I are long overdue for a very important conversation."

8

GWEN

Unfortunately for me, when four thirty rolled around, Atticus was still on a call. Andrew tried to stop me at the door, but I gave him a harsh shake of my head and let myself into my husband's office.

His brows lifted when he saw me, even more so when I locked the door. But he stayed on his call, only watching me warily as I stalked toward him.

He covered the mouthpiece and whispered, "Hey, love, I'm going to be on this call a minute. Is it urgent?"

I nodded, perching myself on the edge of his desk. One thing I could always count on with Atticus was that his desk was going to be pristine. His giant monitor, his pens, pencils, and keyboard, a file for incoming and outgoing mail, and that was it.

And now you.

"I'll wait," I whispered back.

His brows furrowed as if he could tell that I was up to something but wasn't sure quite what or how it was going to affect him. But he kept talking and asking questions about expected projections and future plans for some technology.

I watched his profile as he spoke. The jaw that had been chiseled by the gods, the full lips. His patrician nose. The deep-set wintergreen eyes of his that I had grown to love. The way they were framed and nestled by thick, sooty lashes that were even curlier than mine.

God, I loved this man. My gaze traced over his neck and his Adam's apple that moved and bobbed as he spoke.

I had to press my thighs together to quell some of the throbbing. Before Atticus, I rarely thought about sex. It never even entered into my mind. I always thought maybe I was demisexual or something. I just was never particularly interested.

After Atticus, apparently it was *all* I thought about it.

I shifted slightly, parting my thighs and allowing my skirt to rise up a couple of inches. That caught his attention. His eyes darted to my knees, stayed there for just a moment, and then darted away. It was the tick of his jaw that told me I had him.

I opted to try something.

And what if he rejects you again?

So what if he did? I knew he wanted me. And he was my

Chapter 8

husband, so I wasn't just going to give up. We needed to get over this hump.

I silently snorted a laugh to myself, earning me a lifted brow from him. And his gaze dipped back to my bare legs.

This time, as he spoke on the phone, I parted my legs wider, hiking my skirt up just a little bit more.

This time his gaze lasted longer, and his tongue peeked out to lick his lower lip.

I slid my hand up my thigh, pushing my skirt up higher. With some maneuvering, I hooked the thumb of my good arm in my panties, wiggling and pushing to get them off.

Despite still murmuring his assent on the phone, his gaze was pinned to the juncture of my thighs as I shimmied my panties down my legs and kicked them into his lap. His eyes widened slightly as he noted how soaked they were, but he still didn't take himself off the call.

I hooked one leg around him and let my thighs fall apart. I could feel my arousal trickle down my inner thigh, and so help me, I wanted him to see it. Wanted him to know just how much he affected me.

For a moment, he didn't say anything, but his voice was decidedly huskier when he spoke. "I need those numbers from you first thing in the morning. You're right, we need to prioritize that merger."

I slid my hand down between my thighs, coating my index finger in the wetness between my lips.

His gaze was fixed on my fingers, his brow furrowing

slightly even as he continued his call with gritted teeth. My heart pounded madly in my chest. I had never done anything this bold before, but the idea of Atticus watching me, of showing him just how much I wanted him... It was intoxicating.

"Yes," he said into the receiver, his voice low and tense. "Run those numbers for me."

My finger circled around my sensitive nub, eliciting a quiet gasp from my lips. Atticus never broke his gaze away from my actions, and his eyes darkened with desire and surprise. He was still talking through the phone, although his voice was lower, raspier.

As my fingers dipped lower, making contact with my arousal, my breath hitched. My fingers moved rhythmically, creating pleasurable sensations that left me whimpering in need. Atticus's gaze was glued to my movements, watching as I let myself go under his watchful eyes, his desire evident there.

Atticus seemed momentarily stunned into silence, and I reveled in it. His hand on the receiver was shaking slightly, and he cleared his throat before continuing with the call in a rather strained voice, but his wintergreen eyes never left me.

"All right then, Joshua," he managed to say without stuttering too much. "I expect that report on my desk tomorrow."

His free hand grabbed the edge of the desk so hard that his knuckles turned white as he watched me pleasure myself on his pristine desk. He was barely holding onto his compo-

Chapter 8

sure as I moaned softly under my breath, falling deeper into the sensations.

I slid a second finger inside me and started to slide them in and out, mimicking the way he would fuck me.

With a final goodbye, Atticus hurriedly concluded the call and tossed the phone aside without a second thought.

"Gwen." He breathed out my name as if it were a prayer. "Goddammit. What in the hell are you trying to do to me?" he growled, his voice guttural with arousal.

I bit my lip teasingly as I looked at him through hooded lids before I whispered, "Take a guess."

Ignoring him for a moment longer, I continued to touch myself until I reached the edge then stopped abruptly.

My chest was heaving, my eyes half-lidded with desire when I finally met his, resulting in electric tension between us.

I had him. He was walking the edge of control.

"Will you make me finish on my own, Atticus? Or will you help me?"

His eyes flicked down to the hand between my thighs. A muscle in his clenched jaw worked visibly as he battled with himself. He leaned back in his chair, his hands gripping the armrests so hard that his knuckles were turning white.

"God, Gwen," he breathed, his voice ragged with desire and conflict.

I watched him, my gaze moving from his conflicted face down to the bulge straining against his tailored trousers.

Slowly, I leaned forward, my foot shifting to his chest, and I brushed my fingers over his lips before sitting back and bringing myself back to the edge. With a sharp groan, Atticus inhaled sharply, licking my essence off his lips and closing his eyes as if in agony.

Seeing Atticus lose control like this spurred me on even more. And for the first time in a long time, we both understood each other perfectly. He couldn't hide from me.

Pushing me away wasn't going to work. Creating distance wasn't going to work. I wasn't going to accept this chasm between us.

He couldn't put me on a pedestal. I was flesh and blood. His *wife*. Some very real things had happened to me. To us. And he was going to have to deal with me.

No more hiding.

He moved in closer until he was between my legs, his breath heavy with desire. I leaned back on his desk, my fingers slipping away from their previous position and landing softly on the wood, still glistening.

"Tell me, Gwen," he whispered against my lips, his hands gripping my thighs tightly. "Who do you belong to?"

His voice was silky in its command, sultry and dripping with restrained desire. My heart pounded in my chest, the air between us crackling with electricity.

"You," I whispered back, my voice barely audible but the meaning clear as day. His breath hitched at my surrender, his grip on my thighs tightening.

Chapter 8

"Say it again," he commanded, his lips grazing mine tantalizingly but not meeting them fully. The tease was agonizing and sent tremors through me. His eyes were ablaze with a fire that mirrored my own.

I lifted my chin. "No. You tell me. Who do *you* belong to?"

He lifted a brow, but then his gaze softened. "You have owned me body and soul from the moment I first saw you."

"Then show me. This thing you've been doing… It has to stop now. I'm your wife. Your partner. I will not break."

He swallowed hard. "Gwen, I—"

I shook my head. "No, Atticus. I'm serious." I need you to hear me. "No more. Full partner, at work, at home. No more kid gloves."

His brows furrowed, and he swallowed hard.

"I-I understand, Gwen," he murmured, gently releasing my thighs to cup my face in his hands. His expression was one of both reverence and remorse. "You're right. I've been distant, distracted. In a futile attempt to protect you, I ended up hurting you."

His lips grazed along my neck before moving to my shoulder and then lower still. His breath was hot against my skin as he whispered sweet promises that sent shivers down my spine.

He met my gaze again, his eyes searching mine for any hesitation or signs of discomfort, anything that would make him stop. But I met him head on, my expression determined and wanting. "Atticus," I breathed out. "Don't stop."

His fingers traced along the edge of my skirt before slowly hitching it up, revealing more of me to his hungry gaze.

His other hand still cupped my face as he leaned in closer until his forehead rested against mine.

I swallowed hard as his eyes locked onto mine with a desperate rawness that mirrored my own. "Make me yours, Atticus," I whispered.

Slowly, he lowered his head, his lips brushing against mine in a featherlight kiss before trailing down my jawline and along my neck. His hands firmly spread my legs as he lowered himself, leaving me completely bare for him.

His tongue flicked across my navel before dipping even lower. My breath hitched as his warm mouth and talented tongue found my core. He groaned his approval into the wet heat of my center. "I've missed this," he growled. "Missed tasting all of you, Gwen. You're so fucking delicious."

The vibrations of his voice against my wet folds sent shivers down my spine. My back arched involuntarily, my legs wrapping themselves around his neck as he continued to lavish attention on me. His tongue traced the length of me, swirling in circles, dipping inside before pulling away only to repeat the teasing motions over again.

"Atticus," I moaned, gripping the edge of the desk as my toes curled behind his back. His name fell from my lips like a prayer, a plea for him not to stop as he added his fingers into the mix, sliding one inside me while his thumb circled where I needed it most.

"God, Gwen, your taste, your scent, it's intoxicating," Atticus groaned against me. He looked up at me with hooded eyes filled with lust and desire before descending on me once more, flicking my nub with his tongue as he thrust two fingers inside me. When a third tickled the pucker of my ass, I gasped.

My hips bucked involuntarily against him as he pushed his third finger inside me slowly and gently. "Mm, there's that reaction," he chuckled against my core, causing vibrations to resonate through me. "My filthy little lioness loves it when I play with her ass. Fuck, you love it even more when I fuck this perfect ass, don't you?"

"Yes," I gasped out, the words barely audible over the sound of my own labored breathing. "Yes, Atticus. Please, don't stop."

He gave one final tease before eagerly diving back into me, his tongue flicking and swirling around my core as he began to push his fingers in and out of me with more intensity. His touch was both rough and gentle at the same time, driving me to the edge of insanity.

I felt a familiar tension building within me, a heat that started from my core and was quickly spreading throughout my body. The room started to spin as wave after wave of pleasure washed over me.

"Atticus!" I cried out, arching my back as my climax hit. My body convulsed under his touch, every nerve ending on fire.

He didn't pull away but instead rode out the waves with me, his tongue and fingers continuing their relentless assault even as I writhed beneath him. His actions prolonged the euphoria, making it linger for what felt like an eternity.

My vision grayed out as he shifted his fingers to penetrate my ass with two. "Fuck, yes. That's so good, Ness. I love the way you come for me like a good wife. Especially your tight little ass. Tonight, I'm going to bathe you in my cum. Understand? You're throat, your tits, that pretty pussy. But mostly, your ass. I'm going to watch as you take all of me. I'm going to enjoy pushing any cum that leaks out of your ass back in with my fingers."

Atticus's words hung heavy in the air, a promise of the night to come, my body already buzzing in anticipation as I lay spent on his desk. His voice was the husky purr of an apex predator basking in the afterglow of his conquest, and the reality of it sent another wave of desire crashing through me.

"Understood," I panted out, possessive satisfaction lighting up my gaze as I stared up at him. My husband was staking his claim just as much as I was staking mine.

"Good girl," he whispered before harshly sucking on my clit, sending me back over the edge of oblivion again.

"Holy – Atticus!" I screamed, my voice echoing in the

room as another wave of pleasure crashed over me. He chuckled against me, his laughter vibrating through me and intensifying the sensations.

"You wanted me to lose control. It's gone. Now give me another one before my next call. Just one more, love. Just for me, please."

I wasn't going to make it. Leave it to Atticus to turn this into a power play. "No more. Too sensitive. Please."

"Are you asking me to stop, Ness?" he asked with a soft stroke of his tongue over my clit.

Holy hell, it was good. So good. "I-I don't think I can. I—"

"Just one more," he cooed in a tone that held both command and reassurance. His fingers twisted, hitting the sweet spot inside me that made my body convulse. His mouth descended on me again, creating a vortex of pleasurable sensations.

I could hardly breathe as the tension built up once more. My vision again blurred, my mind clouded with lust and desire. I clung to him desperately, my nails digging into his scalp as I approached the precipice once more.

"You're almost there, Gwen," he murmured against me, his words pushing me closer to my release. "Let go for me."

And just like that, I came undone beneath him. My body thrashed, cries of ecstasy spilling from my lips as waves of pleasure racked through me. My body was on fire, every nerve ending aflame with pleasure.

"There we go," he said in satisfaction, his voice a husky growl against my skin. "God, you're so beautiful when you come."

I lay there panting and trembling, my heart pounding in my chest as the last vestiges of my climax rippled through me.

Gently he eased his fingers from me and pulled back. "I'm going to get you a washcloth and clean you up. But you are going to stay just like that for me while I take my next call. You never know when I'll get hungry again."

9

ATTICUS

As the elevator shot me up the forty-five floors to my penthouse, I rolled my shoulders to release the tension, knowing Gwen was inside.

I scowled at my cock as it immediately strained against my trousers.

"Down, asshole. I need to talk to her first." What had happened in the office had been... unexpected. We still had some things to talk about. It would be helpful if I didn't have her taste lingering on me.

What she'd done in my office... Fuck me.

You mean, the hottest shit you have ever experienced in your life?

That too.

I'd made her stay with her pussy open to me for thirty minutes until it was clear that the phone meeting was going to go on longer. Then I'd made sure the security team had taken her home.

It hadn't been any easier to concentrate though. Not with the taste of her pussy on my tongue.

She'd made a good point today. I had been trying to push her away. Well, not *away* necessarily. I'd been trying to protect her. Keep her safe. My obsession with her and the need to have her in my life had put her at risk, and I hoped to God I could protect her. But because I was so dickmatized by my fucking wife, I'd missed something crucial the day she got shot. There was no getting around that.

Don't be an asshole. She wants you. You want her.

The doors to the elevator slid open. I used the biometric eye scanner and then the additional security gate slid right open too.

I tossed my keys in the little bowl in the vestibule and strolled into the dining room. I knew Micah wasn't here. I'd left him at the office working on a list of proposals for the Vegas Tech Conference in a couple of months, so we had the house to ourselves. And I'd asked Magda to leave food and given her the rest of the night off, so I was surprised when I didn't immediately find Gwen anywhere.

But when I strolled by the library, assuming she was in that room, I found her in the corner, tucked up on the settee, blankets around her, glowering at her laptop. I leaned into the doorframe, staring at her for several long moments, taking her in.

Chapter 9

The moonlight hit her dark skin, highlighting all of the high points and making them glow. I noted the way her teeth grazed her bottom lip as she gnawed on it. The set of her eyes, her hair, tucked up into a messy pile of curls. I wanted to let them down. She'd started wearing it longer now, ever since the Winston Isles.

Maybe it was because of the way you responded to the curls.

Who the fuck knew? I just knew that I wanted to sink my hands in her hair again and tug. Feed my cock to her once again and have her...

"Are you going to stand there all night, or are you going to come in?"

I cleared my throat. "Hey, yourself."

She grinned at me then. "Hello, Mr. Price."

The grin tugged at my lips automatically. "Hello, Mrs. Price."

We both froze, smiling at each other like this was some kind of first date. I had no idea what to say to her. *Sorry I've been a prick and trying desperately not to fuck you. Also, I'm sorry I almost got you killed. And would you please, pretty fucking please, let me taste you like earlier?*

Gwen's brows lifted. "Are you okay?"

"Yeah, I'm fine. Are you okay? How's your shoulder?"

She rolled her eyes and then guiltily slid her gaze to where her sling lay on the coffee table. "In all fairness, I wore it all day. I wanted to have some freedom of movement, and it doesn't hurt so much anymore. It's just not comfy constantly having it tucked against my side."

"You're supposed to wear it."

"There are a lot of things I'm *supposed* to do. Don't be grumpy about it."

"I'm not *grumpy*."

She crossed her eyes at me. "I think that's your grumpy face."

And of course, just like that, she could make me laugh.

"You're being a brat," I said.

"Yes, I am. I feel like you made bold pronouncements this afternoon," she reminded me.

Fuck me. My cock was like a steel bar in my trousers, and I cleared my throat. "Are we going to talk about it?"

She sighed and closed her laptop, tucking the blanket even tighter around herself, like a cocoon of protection.

I joined her on the settee, lifting her feet up onto my lap to massage them.

She released a low groan that immediately made me want to suck on her toe to see what would happen, but I behaved. Because before I could bend her over the end of the settee and fuck her the way I was dying to, we did need to talk.

"Are you mad about this afternoon?" she asked.

I watched her closely. She'd forced me to see I was an idiot. How could she think I was mad? "I'm not mad, Gwen. Why do you think so?"

Chapter 9

"Because I can't read you. I used to be able to. Hell, a few weeks ago, I could tell everything you were thinking just by looking at you. And it's not like you'd give a lot away because, well, you're Atticus. You give nothing away. Literally. I'm consulting runes half the time, and I haven't been able to read you over the last several days. It feels weird. You've gotten really good at shutting me out, and I don't like it."

"I'm not trying to shut you out, Gwen. It's just like I said; I'm scared to death of losing you. Everything that happened..." I shook my head, trying to find the right words to make her understand that this had nothing to do with her, but more about who she was to me.

"I miss you, Atticus." She watched me, waiting for me to continue and say something else.

"I needed you, and I just..." I sighed. "You're right. You're always right, which is annoying, but I needed you and I pushed you away. I've been trying to reconcile and figure this out on my own. And yes, I thought you'd be better, *safer*, if I just didn't touch you." Her brows furrowed and I could see her gearing up for an argument. "I think that was wrong now."

"You *think* that was wrong?"

I sighed. "I know that was wrong. And after what happened in the office..." I narrowed my gaze at her, trying to assess if there was something I could do to make it happen again. "It was like, I don't know, freedom?"

Her brows furrowed, and Christ, all I wanted to do was

kiss her. Just wrap her in my arms and do nothing but kiss her for hours on end. She looked so damn cute. But instead, I continued explaining. "All I've wanted to do for the past several days is to hold you and kiss your fears away, and well, very selfishly, sink into you until I could be certain that you were real. That you were okay. But today, it felt like maybe you *were* okay, and I was caught up in my own bullshit."

She reached a hand out for one of mine, and I gave it to her. "I've needed you, Atticus. Just *you*. Not my billionaire husband. Not the solver of all my problems. Not the man who would burn the whole world down for me. I need the man who insists that I can't eat gummy bears for dinner. The man who, every morning, won't wake me up until I'm waking up on my own just because he likes to watch me sleep. Which is creepy, but you know, we all have weird things. I want the man who wrote me letters even though he knew I was angry with him. I want the man who sends me smoothies to make sure that I eat something other than the aforementioned gummy bears. Not having you felt like I was abandoned, adrift and alone. I don't like feeling like that, Atticus. That's how I felt most of my life before I met you."

I cursed under my breath. "Gwen."

She held up a hand. "I'm serious. I love you. I think I will always love you. I can't be without you. I don't know how to do that, nor in fact, do I want to even try. Just having you not with me, pushing me away, that sucked. I hated it. It felt like I was unwanted, that I was secondary."

Chapter 9

I winced hearing it. That wasn't how I wanted her to feel. It wasn't what I wanted her to think. How could she not know how much I loved her?

"I fucked up, huh?"

She shrugged. "Only a little. And there are ways to make it up to me."

I grinned at her. "Of course, whatever my queen desires, I shall endeavor to rectify my own stupidity because of my terror and fear of losing you."

Her smile was soft. "Well, I mean, this is a pretty easy solution, I think."

"Oh yeah? Let me guess; it starts with this foot massage and ends with you coming around my tongue?"

"The foot massage is a good start, but I'm actually working on something, so the orgasms are going to have to wait."

"You're serious?"

"Yes. I see that my favorite soldier is ready, willing, and available for service. And as much as I want to make use of him, because I have missed you like you would not believe, I'm onto something right now."

I frowned. "Okay, what are you up to?" I scooted myself closer so that her legs bracketed mine like a tent. I used the new position to move my hand up her thighs, and she sucked in a sharp breath.

"Atticus, you cannot distract me right now."

I shrugged. "What? I finally understand that if I touch

my wife I'm not going to be hurting her, and now you want to stop me?"

"I don't want to stop you, but focus first. I think I hacked into the cameras in the garage across the street."

If that wasn't an ice-bucket bath, I didn't know what was. "What the hell are you doing?"

"Easy does it. Remember, you weren't going to go crazy on me and act overly protective."

You just promised. "Um, right."

"I think I may have video footage of whoever shot me."

"Holy shit. Can you show me?"

She opened her laptop again. "Okay, so this is our building in this model I've made, yeah? And these are the office buildings across the way." She pointed out the window. "That's the parking structure two-blocks down, right? Across the street from it, there's a building under construction."

She pulled up a video on her laptop then showed me as I strained to glare at the dark grimy footage. She paused it and then pointed. "See? Right there. The cameras appear to move around. They're constantly in rotation. If they were a pro, they would have known and maybe disabled the cameras, or maybe they just left that one, I have no idea. But look, you can see it. They come up the stairs, and then right there, you can see them as they get into position."

She was right, they did get into position as if seemingly looking down the street, as if *expecting* us. Like we had come home at exactly the time that was anticipated.

Chapter 9

How had they known exactly when to expect us?

Again, we watched the dark grimy figure line up the shot. Then we saw two flares from the rifle. *Two*. Had one gone wide?

I wanted that damn bullet. I might be able to track them from the ammunition that they'd used.

"And then it doesn't show any cars leaving or anyone coming out. There are no cameras to access on the other side of the building, but the way I figure it, if we just take to the street, we'll find someone who was around that day. Maybe someone unhoused. Maybe a security guard. We have no way of knowing, but I figure we can at least start hitting the pavement and look."

I stared at her, shaking my head. "How did you do this?"

"I didn't do anything."

"Yes, you did. Because we assumed, given the direction, that the shots came from the building across the street."

"I mean, you're not *entirely* wrong, but because that building is under construction, the elevators were inaccessible. Whoever it was deliberately climbed the stairs or figured out how to make the service elevator run. They were determined."

"The question is, why?"

"And, the other question," she added, "is who that person was. And can we talk to them?"

10

ATTICUS

AN HOUR LATER, Gwen hesitated in the doorway as I lay back against the headboard of our bed. She had taken quite a while getting ready for bed, and I tried not to focus on the sling on her left arm.

"Come here, Gwen."

She shifted from foot to foot, peering up at me through her lashes. And fuck, all I wanted to do was jump out of bed, dig my hands into her hair, and worship her until she was melting. And then I wanted to throw her on the bed and spread her pussy out like the smorgasbord that it would be.

But it wasn't her fault that I was barely holding on to my control. It was mine. I promised myself I'd take it easy and go slow.

She slowly walked over to her side of the bed, sliding in, and I noticed under that little camisole thing that she wore to bed she didn't have on any panties. She turned off her light and rolled over toward me. "I'm here. Is there something you wanted?"

I stared at her for a moment in the dim light, my gaze tripping over the bridge of her nose, the full ripeness of her lips, the smile that hovered at the corners. My heart squeezed. She was mine. All mine. And she wanted to be here. More importantly she wanted *me* in here. So why was I nervous?

"There's a lot that I want."

I shifted position to place her against the pillows in the center of the bed. Then I drew back the covers and blankets until she was exposed in front of me. "I think I'm going to start at the feet and work my way up."

Gwen's breath caught as I moved down the bed, grasping her ankle gently and lifting her leg. I pressed a kiss to the arch of her foot, my eyes never leaving hers.

"I want you to know, Gwen," I murmured, my fingers massaging the curve of her heel, "this isn't just about tonight. This is about every night. Every morning. Every stolen afternoon. And also about every moment I've missed. Every moment I plan to make up for."

She gasped as I flicked my tongue against her ankle, tasting the saltiness of her skin. Her eyes fluttered closed, and she bit her lower lip in anticipation as I continued my slow, torturous ascent up her leg.

"I want you to remember tonight," I said, pressing kisses

up along her calf. "I want you to remember the feel of my hands on your skin, my breath against your thigh." I nipped lightly at the inside of her knee, eliciting a shuddering breath from Gwen. "I want you to remember that you belong to me."

Her hands clenched and fisted the sheets as I teased my way higher, my lips tracing a path along the inside of her thighs. She was so soft and warm, and she smelled of honey and woman and something uniquely Gwen. The heady scent intoxicated me, fueling the fire in my belly.

As my lips trailed higher, I couldn't help but marvel at the way her body trembled beneath my touch. It was as if she'd been waiting for this moment as much as I had. Our time apart had left us both aching, longing. And now, we were finally here, together again.

"Atticus," she whispered, her voice thick with need.

"Shh," I soothed, flicking my tongue along her inner thigh. "Just feel."

I could feel her muscles clench and unclench as I neared her core, the scent of her arousal filling the air. Her wetness served to only further incite my own hunger, but tonight was about her. Tonight was about making up for all the nights we'd missed, all the touches we'd yearned for.

Finally, I reached the apex of her thighs and looked up at her. "Gwen," I breathed, my voice a low growl. "Tonight, I'm going to taste every inch of you. Every. Inch."

Her response was a strangled moan as I dipped my head

between her thighs, spreading them wide with my hands and using my shoulders to keep them open.

With another smirk up at her, I planted my mouth over her pussy. Her taste exploded across my tongue, and I groaned low in satisfaction.

I teased her folds with my tongue, swirling and flicking, drinking in her essence. Gwen's hips arched upward in response, her fingers digging into the sheets as moans and whimpers spilled from her lips.

"That's it," I purred against her core. "Let it out, Ness. I want to hear every sound."

Her indrawn breath was like music to my ears as I lapped at her folds, tasting the sweet nectar of her arousal. Slowly, I teased my way up her slit, savoring every inch of her until I reached the sensitive bud of her clit.

Her response was a cry ripped from deep within her chest as I plunged two fingers into her wet core. Her hips bucked, riding my fingers as they thrust inside her. All the while, I never stopped my oral assault on her clit, dragging her straight to the edge of oblivion.

Her fingers latched into my hair, tugging me close while she ground her sweet cunt against my face. Fuck me, I was never leaving. I would spend the rest of my life right here, between her firm thighs.

When I pulled one of my now-slick fingers from her pussy and teased her tight starfish entrance with it, she choked out a sob. "Oh God, Atticus."

"Yeah, baby. I'm going to keep my promise to you and fuck you here. Would you like that, Ness? Tell me how much you want it."

Her body trembled beneath me, and her eyes squeezed tight as my slick finger traced around her entrance. "I want it," she gasped, her hands tightening in my hair. "Atticus, please."

I gently pressed my slick finger against her tight opening, teasing her. I wanted to drive her to the edge of madness and then pull her back just before she fell over the ledge. Tonight was about savoring every moment, not rushing into anything.

Slowly but surely, I eased the tip of my finger past her entrance. She gasped at the intrusion but didn't protest. The look in her eyes was one of unadulterated pleasure mixed with anticipation.

As I slowly pushed deeper inside, she whimpered softly and bit down on her lower lip. Her hips rose from the bed, pushing against my hand in a silent plea for more.

"Look at me," I ordered hoarsely as I plunged deeper. Gwen's eyes met mine, and the intensity of her gaze lit a fire within me that only she could extinguish.

With agonizing slowness, I pulled my finger back before pushing forward again, burrowing deeper into her ass with each thrust. Her breath hitched every time I moved further inside her; a mixture of gasps and moans filled the room along with the rustle of soft sheets beneath us.

Letting go of her clit, I placed my other hand on her

Chapter 10

lower stomach, pressing down with the heel of my palm, applying just enough pressure to make her pant and twitch.

"Are you close, Ness? Does my beautiful wife want to come?"

"Yes, yes," she gasped out between pants, her body starting to shake. Her grip on my hair didn't slacken, instead pulling me in even closer.

With a smile, I pulled back, easing my tongue and fingers out of her. She made a whimpering plea as I gently eased off her sling before maneuvering her onto her stomach, grabbing a pillow to place under her so her ass was on perfect display for me.

My eyes roamed her flawless form, taking in the sight of her arched back, the curvature of her hips, and the succulent, juicy apple of her ass. Her clenched fists gripped tightly to the sheets as she awaited my next move. The anticipation in the room was thick enough to cut through with a knife.

My hand trailed up her thigh, pausing to give her ass a firm squeeze before I dipped my finger into her wet heat once more. She gasped, arching her back to meet my touch as I slid another finger deeper inside her. I slowly pumped in and out, my other hand moving to caress the span of her back.

Sweating lightly from the heat of our bodies, I leaned over her figure, my chest pressing into the smooth plane of her back. My lips found their way to the nape of her neck, kissing and biting softly while my fingers kept thrusting within her warmth.

One of my hands moved upward, cupping one of her pert breasts while I continued to suckle at her neck. She twisted underneath me, angling herself so that I had better access to all of her sensitive spots.

"Atticus," she muttered in a breathless sigh as my thumb began rubbing circles around her nipple, pinching it until it peaked.

"Yes, love?" I murmured against the shell of her ear.

She groaned at my teasing tone and tried to push herself onto my fingers. "Quit teasing and fuck me."

A chuckle escaped me before I kissed a path down to her ass, nipping her skin gently as I traveled. "Patience," I murmured against her skin before flicking my tongue down the seam of her ass.

With my free hand, I grasped her cheek, holding her open as I licked her ass and fucked her pussy with my fingers.

"Oh, fuck!" she moaned, her entire body shaking as I continued to press against her most sensitive spots.

"I can't wait to come inside this tight hole," I growled against her skin before leaning in to taste the scent of her arousal.

When I pulled back once again, this time to get the lube and shuck my boxers, Gwen shook beneath me.

I coated my thick erection as I watched her writhe

Chapter 10

against the pillow. "Baby, are you trying to get yourself off on that pillow?"

"No," she whispered, then changed her answer. "Yes," she said with a squeak.

I landed a palm swiftly on her ass, and she made a sound that was part moan, part plea, and all arousal. "Naughty wife. Tonight your orgasm belongs to me, remember? You wanted me to remember how good we are together. And I want you to remember whose pussy and ass this is. I want my orgasms. Do you hear me?"

She gasped and nodded, her hands clenching the sheets once more. "Yours, all yours."

"Good girl," I purred, bringing the mushroom tip of my cock to her ass. With one slow push I entered her tight heat. *Oh fuuuuck.* The edges of my vision went gray, and I felt dizzy for a moment.

Through clenched teeth, I asked. "Ness, you okay?"

"God... yes," she groaned as I slid inch by torturous inch into her tightest hole. She was so damn perfect, so wet and hot and tight that it took every ounce of my control to go slow.

Her inner muscles spasmed around me as I bottomed out. The wave of pleasure that washed over me made my knees weak and my balls tighten.

Slowly, I started to pull out before slamming back in. She arched her back, taking me deeper while she moaned my name.

"You feel so fucking good," I growled out as I started a slow, deep rhythm. "Fuck, you feel so tight and hot around me. You're mine, all mine."

"Yes, yes!" she groaned, pushing back against me.

Her hands clawed at the sheets as she met me thrust for thrust, her moans spurring me on. My grip on her hips tightened, hoping not to bruise her delicate skin, but I couldn't help it. The sight of my cock disappearing into her ass before reappearing was enough to make me lose my mind.

"Oh God, Atticus, I'm so close!"

"Let go, baby. I have you. I always have you." And with those words, her body convulsed around my cock.

I continued to thrust into her while her orgasm rocked through her shaking body.

"That's it, come for me," I growled out, my own orgasm cresting.

With a final thrust, I came deep within her tight heat, marking her as mine completely.

Breathing heavily, I collapsed on top of her, my cock still buried deep within her ass. "Fuck, Ness..." was all I managed to get out. I didn't know how long we stayed like that, but I eventually eased out of her then headed to the bathroom. I turned the faucets on in the tub and grabbed a few wet washcloths for her.

"Here, baby," I said, cleaning her up before I picked her up and carried her to the bathroom.

"Atticus, I can walk you know."

Chapter 10

Gently I placed her in the tub before sliding in behind her. "I'm aware. But I have a massage to complete. Somebody distracted me."

"Oh, that was me, was it?"

"Sure was." I kissed her neck again. "I'm sorry I was a fool. I won't pull back from you anymore."

"Glad to hear it. Now that you're being reasonable, maybe we can talk about what the hell you did with my job."

11

GWEN

"Don't you think this is a little extra?"

I glowered at Atticus as he double and triple-checked my bulletproof vest.

The compromise was three of Pierce's men. He'd wanted five for a simple excursion across the street.

"Somebody shot at you right from that building," he reminded me. "You would think that maybe you'd remember that."

"Yes, I do remember." I rolled my shoulder again. "However, the vest in broad daylight is a bit much, right?"

"I don't know, because I don't know who shot you," he said, trying to sound perfectly logical. "Stop being stubborn. Let me do this."

I searched his gaze, and I could see the stress around his eyes and his mouth, so I stopped arguing.

Chapter 11

And not that I had a death wish or anything, but we were literally just crossing the street and going down a block. But he had a point. We didn't know who had tried to shoot me. So it was probably better to be safe than sorry.

"Fine. But do we really need all three of them, or would one suffice?"

"Yes, all three."

"If you saw a random couple approaching you with three massive dudes behind them, would you talk to them?" I asked.

He frowned, inclining his head at Sven. "Sven, you're with us. You two stay back a bit."

The others didn't look pleased about it. And for that matter, neither did Sven. But it didn't matter, because at least I had my husband back. That shell of a man who'd been walking around the house since I'd gotten home from the hospital was gone. And I was glad because I wasn't particularly fond of him.

He took my hand and we crossed the street, deftly managing to avoid the puddles from the rain the night before. "Are you okay?"

"Yes, Atticus, I'm fine."

"Are you sure? Because you winced just now."

I snorted out an exhausted laugh. "I winced because someone was a little greedy in the shower this morning and had to fuck me twice."

He smiled contritely, but I could see the hint of mischief in his eyes. "Well, I'm trying to make up for lost time."

"Yes, and I appreciate it. But I'm sore, so sometimes I'm going to wince a little. Especially when we're skipping over puddles."

"Okay, I promise, I'll take it easy the next couple of days."

"You will do no such thing, Atticus Price. Matter of fact, I might demand another shower this afternoon."

"Oh? Well, my wife *is* greedy."

About five feet behind us, Sven just cleared his throat and tried to look anywhere but at us. I shook my head at him and grinned at Atticus. "Let's go."

My thoughtful husband slowed his normal pace down for me and shortened his stride slightly so I could keep up. When we reached the construction site, he found the foreman. "Hey, just a random question. We had a security issue a couple of weeks back. Any chance you have security guards who are supposed to be watching the place at night?"

The foreman frowned. "What's this about?"

Atticus opened his mouth, but I thought maybe we would try the honey approach first. I slid a hand on his chest gently and patted it. "What my husband is trying to say is, we noticed from the security camera from the other building that there was somebody stationed kind of in the door frame, and we were just wondering if they saw anyone coming or going. Anyone running away from the building on either side that night?"

Chapter 11

The foreman frowned as he looked at me, then back at Atticus, then back at me again. I gave him a dazzling smile that hopefully said, 'Please help us, so that my husband doesn't make you regret your life choices.'

The guy nodded and went over to his laptop, typing something in. "Um, you're looking for Adam Bailey. Luckily for you, he is on shift right now. Just down that way. Watch your head." He pointed to another man standing off to the side. "Troy over there, he'll take you down to the security room."

I gave Atticus a wide grin, and he looked like, well, like perhaps he wanted to spank me. But that wasn't the point. The point was, I'd gotten us what we needed.

As we marched through the security office with our hardhats on, Sven hilariously made it look like his could easily scrape the ceiling. Atticus just shook his head at me. "I'm just worried about you, that's all."

"I'm fine. And he's willing to talk to us. See? You don't have to break down everything."

"It's more efficient though, isn't it?"

I rolled my eyes. "When did I become the warm and fuzzy one?"

He laughed at that. "Is that what you're calling this? Warm and fuzzy?"

"I'm calling it being good with people," I smirked.

When we reached the security office, we found Adam Bailey, and Sven parked himself outside the room.

"Excuse us?" Atticus said tentatively.

Bailey turned around and nodded, eyeing me, then Atticus. "Yeah? What can I help you with?"

Atticus stepped forward. "On the night of August eighth, were you on duty?"

He frowned again. "I don't know. If the boss says I was on duty, maybe I was."

I sighed, trying to take over again, but Atticus stopped me. "You see, my wife, she's pretty patient. But somebody tried to shoot her that night, so I'm far *less* patient, right? You were on duty. Your foreman already confirmed for us. Which means you had to have seen someone coming and going, and if you didn't, I bet there was something on these cameras."

He swallowed hard, shifting his gaze. "Look, I didn't do anything. Sometimes I turn a blind eye when a couple of kids come in and smoke or something."

"You let people smoke in this building? Aren't there highly flammable materials around?"

"I don't know. Look, that night, some kid comes up to me and offers me fifty bucks to turn off our back cameras. Of course, I didn't see him again. But when I checked, nothing was taken."

Atticus groaned. "You know what this kid looks like?"

"No. I didn't pay that much attention."

"You don't have a name or anything?"

"No, but I see him around from time to time."

Chapter 11

Atticus looked like he wanted to pummel him as he took another menacing step toward Adam Bailey. I stepped between them. "Sorry about him. He really is particular about my safety. So the kid paid you fifty bucks for you to pay a little less attention to what might be going on inside the building. Nothing was reported missing, and you probably forgot about him. I get that. But if you saw the kid again, could you point him out to us?"

"Yeah, I guess so."

"Okay then." I turned my attention back to Atticus. "We could probably get footage from across the street and see if we can get the kid on camera. Maybe he's local and works around here or something."

Atticus pressed his lips firmly together. "Yeah, maybe."

"Okay, how does that sound, Mr. Bailey? If you'll help us with this, we won't tell your employer you're letting people come in and smoke around flammable materials. Though honestly, really?"

He sighed. "You're not going to rat on me?"

"No, we just want to find this kid. That's it."

Atticus mumbled under his breath. "*I* might rat."

I rolled my eyes. "That's enough out of you."

He groaned low. "Fine. However, we will be getting your details from your employer, Bailey. Don't run, or I will make it my personal job to come and look for you. You won't like it."

The man stared at him as if suddenly hyperaware that

maybe he'd miscalculated somewhere along the way. "Yeah, I got it."

As we left, I took my husband's hand. "Did you have to scare him?"

"If he knows something, he needs to tell us. If I have to scare the information out of him, I'm happy to do so."

"Right. But what if... you know, people are right when they say you catch more flies with honey."

"No one says that. Also, I don't want to catch flies. I want to catch the idiot who tried to kill my wife."

"I know. I know. And I love you."

He dipped and kissed me gently. "Good. I love you too. Now let's get to work. Apparently, I need to resolve a little issue with the whole employee management team."

12

GWEN

I was not looking forward to this. My father was coming in to do the final sign-off on paperwork concerning Atticus's deal with him now that the wedding had been made public. He'd insisted that I be there for the meeting though, which likely meant he was looking for some kind of confrontation. I was loath to give him anything he wanted, but Atticus had wanted me there too. And oddly, when we walked into the conference room, he sat me at the head of the table and took the seat next to me.

When my father walked in, Atticus was all smiles, shook his hand, and invited him to take a seat. My father frowned when he saw where I was sitting. "Well, I suppose congratulations are in order. Though, it would have been nice to know when my own daughter got married. Of course I had to take it upon myself to verify that the wedding was, in fact, completely legal."

Atticus merely shrugged as I scowled, pinching my jaw tighter and tighter until my right molar hurt. As I stared at my father, I tried to make sense of why I had spent so much of my time needing a kind word from him, needing him to see me, needing *anything* from him.

He hadn't always been terrible. There was a time when Mom was still alive that he cared. Or at least he did a reasonable facsimile of caring when he turned up for the occasional recital or to check on me because Mom had said that he should. I wondered when he'd started to hate me. And for a long time, I thought he did. But I realized that so much of this indifference was just a casual selfishness where he only thought of himself first.

Oh, and he's a colorist. But what can you do about that?

Atticus inclined his head to me. "Gwen, why don't you walk your father through the final termination points of his deal?"

I lifted my brow. Atticus knew all the points. He just wanted me to be the one to say it. To put the final nail in my father's coffin. He wanted to give that to me. And it was weird, because I didn't want it, or rather I didn't *need* it anymore. What I saw was a sad old man who was so self-absorbed he denied himself love. The chance to know his daughters.

"Your signature on this line concludes all business that

Chapter 12

Becks has with Pendragon. All the terms of the agreement have been met."

My father tried to bluster. "Now, I haven't verified—"

I put up a hand casually, dismissively. "No, you have the proof. All the paperwork has been filed at the county registrar of New York. Atticus and I are, in fact, legally married. And the portion of Becks technology that you purchased four years ago, has now been transferred to Pendragon. You and I are now separate."

My father eased himself down on the chair and glowered at me. "So what, you think you're important now and you can forget that we are family? I'll see you on Friday night."

I shrugged. "I will only see you on Friday because I care about Clarissa and Morgan. Not because I care about you. And while we're on the subject of our weekly 'family' nights, I will no longer be jumping through hoops for you, and you will start treating Clarissa with respect. I will no longer stand by and let you talk to her however you wish."

"You want to tell me what to do at my own house?"

Atticus grinned at that. "Sweetheart, why don't you tell your father about that fancy little clause in your mother's will that maybe he forgot about?"

I smiled at him then, reveling in Atticus going to bat for me. "Oh, yes. At the time it wasn't a concern because I wasn't ever planning on getting married. But you do remember Mom's little stipulation before you wed? That when she got married, *she'd* become the owner of the house, and then of course, upon her death the house went back into trust for her daughters. And whoever got married first was to have it as her family home."

Dad started to turn red under his skin. "What are you talking about? That's my house."

"Correction, Dad, that is now *my* house. Now, I'm inclined to let you live there for as long as you choose to do so, but from now on, I'm going to allow Clarissa to do whatever she wants with the house. Morgan too. The two of them shall decide, since they'll be spending the majority of the time there. Not you. You'll make no more decisions about what can and cannot be changed. No more decisions about who can come and go. No more decisions about staff. All of those will be made by Clarissa from now on."

"How dare you? I raised you. I put a roof over your head."

I lifted a finger and waived it at him. "No, technically, grandfather put a roof over my head. But I will give you this; you maintained it. And for a while there, Mom loved you. And from what I remember, you loved her too. I get that it changed you when she died. But what I don't get is how you could look at us, knowing we needed our mother, knowing we needed *you*, and yet you refused to help us. You just poured yourself into your job, into the most expensive bottles of scotch you could find, and replaced my mother like you were trading cars. Thank God we got lucky with Clarissa, but you turned yourself off. You stopped caring. And maybe you never loved me as much as you loved Morgan, but I

Chapter 12

know that you *did* love me once. You took me riding when I was little. I remember that. I remember you holding me on my first pony. When I fell, you came over and held me, firmly but gently, and told me I needed to get back on so that I wouldn't be afraid. You did care. You were just... absent in so many ways. So you can live there as long as you want. You're my dad, after all. But the fact that you were so eager to sell off your daughters makes me less inclined to help you at all."

"Now wait a damn minute, you cannot do this. That is my house."

Atticus pushed to his feet then. "I think we're done here. Gwen has already told you everything you need to know, and she has the benefit of Pendragon lawyers behind her. You'll find that everything is in order. The house is hers. And she's already told you how it's going to be. So you should probably start getting on good terms with your current wife."

Atticus reached his hand out to me, and I smiled up at him, taking it and getting to my feet. "Dad, I hope that one day you recognize the pain and the heartache you put me through for no good reason, though I know it's unlikely. But you know, a girl can't help but dream. And even if you somehow stopped loving me, I do love you. Atticus and I will see you for dinner on Friday."

When I walked out of the conference room, I didn't realize I was shaking until Atticus rubbed gentle circles into my lower back. "How are you doing?" he asked in a quiet voice.

"Um, I feel like I just ran half a mile, flat out."

"Well, that was emotional. So that about covers it."

We nodded at several employees before he pulled me into the stairwell and tucked my face into his chest. He wrapped his arms around me, holding me tight. "You're going to be okay, Gwen."

"I know. I expected that to hurt, to feel something. But all I feel is numb."

"That's probably to be expected. You just did a hard thing. But now it's over, and you only have to see him on your terms from here on out."

"I'm not sure I could have done that without you."

He shrugged. "You didn't really need me."

"Yeah, I did. But I will say it felt damn good. Wait till I tell Clarissa that she can do whatever she wants with the house. She's been itching to redo that study for years."

"Good for her. And that's really generous of you."

"She's my stepmother. I may not have grown up with her because I was almost out of the house by the time she came to live with us, but she's been good with Morgan. And my father is an asshole to her. She doesn't deserve that."

"I wholeheartedly agree." He pressed a kiss to my temple. "Now, let's just go and verify that he can't find some way to retaliate."

13

ATTICUS

Gwen had made herself scarce once I told her the boys were coming around. I assumed she was in the library or the bedroom.

When Pierce showed up with Lance in tow, I frowned. "I swear to God, I'll send you back to London, Lakewood."

Lance just grinned and shrugged. "Nope. Apparently, someone tried to kill my best friend, and I should probably stick around until that's cleared up."

I hated that he was right. While Gwen was in danger, keeping close the people who cared about her and would do their best to protect her was what we needed.

"Are you here for me or for her?"

"Well, I was here to see her. And I will. But Pierce told me that you guys were up to no good, so I figured I should probably check in and make sure you don't blow up her life first."

I ground my teeth. "I still don't like you Lakewood."

"What else is new? But you're currently the guy who's supposed to make sure she doesn't get whacked. I have to check in and make sure you do your job right."

I glowered at Pierce. "Did you have to bring him up?"

"He is on the approved visitor list, but we can take him off." Pierce winked at me. "I never liked him anyway."

Lakewood just grinned at Pierce as he led us both into the study. Gavin, Micah, and Rowan frowned when they saw Lance, but none of them questioned him being there. Micah actually looked slightly entertained by the whole prospect.

"Well, the gang is all here." Lakewood said.

Gavin sat back and took a sip of his scotch. "Hell, if I knew we were adding one more to this boy's club, I would have brought more brownies."

Lakewood immediately went to the plate in the middle of the coffee table before even going for his scotch. Damn it, I'd hoped to save more brownies. But the way this lot ate, there wouldn't be any left.

And Gavin, that fuck, as good as he was at baking, he rarely did it. Only when he had his daughter, Emery, with him. And he and Emery's mother were still working on that custody agreement. At least one that he could live with.

Lance just made himself right at home. I ignored him

Chapter 13

and turned my attention to my brother. "Micah, can't you hack your way into this information?"

"Asking questions like that, I'd swear you don't run a multi-national tech corporation," he said with a chuckle.

"I may run it, but I don't own it anymore, remember? The real juice is in the other room."

Micah muttered under his breath, "Shall I go and ask *her* what we do next?"

"As much as you know she'd love that, the answer is no. This is on us. We fucked up somewhere, so we fix it," I reminded him. "This isn't for her to fix."

Micah nodded. "But to be fair, she did save us from Dad twice. So maybe this is the time to ask."

I hated that I had to tell him the truth. "Well, she's still miffed at me for pulling back all her tasks at Pendragon, so she's deliberately teaching me a lesson and trying to catch up on all the work she missed. You know how Gwen loves her job."

Lakewood shrugged. "If you'd asked, I could have told you not to take her team away from her. It's the number one way to have her dive right back into everything. She once went on vacation for a whole four days and came back early just because she was afraid I was fucking things up."

"Yeah, that sounds about right," I agreed.

"But I know a trick, if you want it. Should I be so bold?" he asked.

I crossed my arms and leaned back against my desk. "Are

you telling me you know my wife better than I do, Lakewood?"

He gave me a shit-eating grin, bit into the brownie, then deliberately tossed the remainder of it in his mouth. "Well, she did run to me in London, didn't she?" he asked around a mouthful of chocolate.

I was off the desk in a second, but Micah planted a firm hand on my chest. Pierce stepped into the pathway too. None of them were going to let me kill him. "What the fuck did you say?" I snarled.

"Oh, easy does it. She married you, asshole. I'm just saying, I do know her well. But by all means, keep carrying on this way. It's entertaining for me when you fuck up."

I could still feel the pressure of my brother's hand on my chest, and I glowered at him. His silent, long look told me I needed to settle down and stop letting Lakewood get to me. I knew he was right. I'd been on edge, and nothing was going the way I had planned or the way I wanted it to. We still had no answers, and Gwen was still in the crosshairs. If I didn't figure out the answers soon, I was going to have to send her away again.

Oh, great. Lakewood is right. You never learn your lessons.

No, this time I'd be going with her. We'd take an extended honeymoon. Somewhere quiet and remote. Somewhere no one knew about. Not even my guys.

She won't like that.

Chapter 13

No, she would not. But if we didn't have something actionable soon, it might be the safer option. Because I knew her. She couldn't live with constant security for long. Constant attention on where she was going and who she was going to be with. It made her sad, and I didn't like that.

"If everyone has settled down now, we need a plan of attack," Rowan said. He also grabbed a brownie, and it was all I could do not to snap at him.

"Where are we on the kid the security guard saw?" I asked.

Rowan nodded and then clicked the remote to the big screen monitor on the wall. "That is Philip Mangles. He works at the garage down the street. His dad owns it, so he's got a little freedom. He got into trouble a while back, nothing major. A couple of possession charges. His crew though, if you can call them that, have all been in and out of jail, a bunch of real lay-abouts. It's a shame too. I hear this kid is a half-decent artist."

I frowned at the kid with scraggly brown hair that looked like it was in desperate need of a cut at the very least, or maybe a shearing to get some of the mats out of it. And was that a face tattoo? "Where do I find him?" I asked Rowan.

"Well, that's the bet. You're as likely to find him around the garage as anywhere else. While he technically lives at home, he never seems to spend any time there. Sven and I tried to pay him a visit there."

I stared at his photo again. "Okay, so you already tried talking to him, but it was a no go?"

Pierce nodded. "Yeah. I've already got a couple of guys watching the garage. As soon as he turns up, we'll grab him."

"Yeah, do that. But don't spook him," I warned. "If you find him, I want a chance to question him first."

Pierce nodded.

"Do we have any other angles?" I asked. "I hate to say it, but could this have been Dad?"

Micah drained his glass at the mention of our father. "I've checked his financials. A job like this would call for money, at least six figures, and I don't see any movements on his accounts that set off alarms."

Hearing the idea that Gwen's life was a matter of zeros made my stomach turn. "And we're sure? Maybe someone is doing him a favor?"

My brother shook his head. "Is he despicable? Yes. Real scum of the earth type, that's our dad. But is he responsible for this through a hired gun? I don't think so unless he's got debts we can't see. He was under the impression that he would be running Pendragon right now. He may have made promises. I'll keep digging."

I pinched the bridge of my nose. At some point, I might have to see to it myself. That's what he wanted, after all, my attention.

"While we're at it, let's pull another background check on Becker too," I suggested.

Chapter 13

Lakewood swiped a hand through his hair. "It doesn't make sense. He needed the deal with you to go through. He had no reason to take her out, his own daughter. I mean, he's a selfish prick, but he doesn't hate her."

"Right now, we have to consider everyone. While we're at it, pull a full background on every single person who's close to her. Let's do it again."

Rowan rubbed the back of his neck and glanced up at Pierce. I caught the look. The one that said that I was grasping at straws here.

"You guys think I don't realize that I'm getting a little desperate?" I asked. "I am. I readily admit it. But the thing is, we don't have *anything*. You guys haven't turned up jack shit."

Pierce cleared his throat. "Easy does it, Atticus."

Gavin just watched the whole thing, sucked in a deep breath, and muttered, "He's right. Check everyone. All of us too."

Lakewood laughed, but Gavin stopped him with a look before he continued. "One of us, at some point, must have come in contact with somebody who knows something, who has *seen* something. We are the closest people to Atticus. If someone is trying to get to him through Gwen, it makes sense to put us under the microscope. Toss everyone that has even looked at Gwen for the last year. She didn't seem to have any trouble directed at her specifically until London. So maybe we start with what happened between the breakup and when Atticus went to get her. Because something changed. And we have to figure out what it was. Anything out of the ordinary, that's what we need to dig through."

I hated to admit it, but he was right. We'd missed something, and we needed to start with the time that I didn't want to think about. What had happened after I broke Gwen's heart? And by sending her away, what the hell did that trigger?

14

GWEN

WHAT WERE they doing in there?

I'd heard laughter and then what sounded like some back-slapping, and then suddenly it sounded tense. Not that I was listening in on their conversations or anything, because that was beneath me. If I wanted to know what was going on, I would just walk in. After all, this was my house, wasn't it?

You're a chicken.

Yes, I was a chicken. And maybe I had invented work I needed to do. I surreptitiously glanced back at my laptop. I did not have that much work to do. I had mostly sorted out Jack and the disarray he'd put my team into already. Got the releases back on track, sewed the ruffled feathers, and I was in control again. Oh, God, it felt good. And Jack... Well, Jack was trying to be what he liked to call *helpful*. But Jack needed to just do the work I had already assigned him.

Next on the docket was looking at all the proposals before the board, and my eyeballs were crossing. This was so important, and I wanted to get it right. The future of the company, hundreds of people, hell, *thousands* across the world were depending on me getting this right, and it just felt like so much pressure. I was slowly pouring through perspectives and getting the lay of the land, but God, every time I sat down to even think about it, my eyeballs started to cross, and all I wanted to do was sleep. But I wasn't telling Atticus that. He had given me his company, every share he had. It was a symbol of trust and love, and I wasn't going to let him down. But he was over there distracting me with all of his friends over. No doubt discussing me. Why didn't I get an invite to the round table meeting?

My phone dinged on my bed, and I did a flying plop to reach it.

Sissy Face: *Where are you?*

Me: *Home, why? Are you doing something fun?*

Sissy Face: *Well, I was meant to be enjoying myself at this lounge, but DJ Akimbo is playing. And it's actually pretty awesome, except dick face is here, and he's staring at me.*

I scrunched my eyes, trying to ascertain which of the guys she'd told me about recently was called dick face. They all had nicknames, but it hurt my head trying to figure out which one had likely pissed her off and got his previous name changed. Like, pizza guy, or bought-me-coffee guy, and now was known as dick face.

Chapter 14

Me: *Sorry, it doesn't ring a bell. Which one?*

Sissy face: *The one dad introduced me to. The one I said was cute. I've changed my mind. He's not cute. He's annoying.*

Me: *Oh, the one who keeps calling you all the time?*

Sissy face: *Yes, him. He's here and staring at me from the bar. He tried to buy me a drink, and I declined. He seemed pissed off, and now he is giving me the creeps.*

Me: *At the risk of sounding like your uncool sister, maybe it's time to leave? Go home.*

Sissy face: *No, it's Lisa's birthday, and we haven't done the cake and shit yet. It's fine. I can manage, but oh God, he really is creeping me out.*

My first instinct was to change and head down to the bar to provide extra protection. Protection that I myself *apparently* needed because somebody was trying to shoot at me, so that wasn't going to work.

But wait... you have six available very large men at your disposal. Hell, technically, tonight, you have nine. There are two more on the elevator downstairs and one in the lobby. You could roll deep.

I stared at my phone again. It would be nothing. I could just go get her.

Except, there's no way Atticus lets you go. And you are likely overreacting.

Was I overreacting though?

Me: *No joke, Morgan, are you scared?*

Sissy Face: *He's come to the table and now he's standing right next to me. I'm really, really uncomfortable.*

Well fuck. I bounced off the bed as I typed.

Me: *Sit tight, we're coming to get you.*

I then marched toward the study in my camisole and short-shorts. I had already taken off my bra, and my shorts look more like boy-cut panties than actual workout shorts, and I could imagine the face that Atticus would make.

I paused briefly to go back and grab sweats to throw on over them, sliding a hoodie over my hair, which just made it look like a rat's nest, but I would fix that later.

I almost knocked on the study door like I didn't live there. But instead, I opened it, poking my head in, and six heads whipped around in my direction. "Gentlemen, sorry to interrupt."

Atticus's face lit up like a Christmas tree. It wasn't so much his smile, which he did give, the slow one that sort of snuck out like a thief in the night and quickly turned into something that looked like he was thinking about the last time he licked me, which was this morning. In the car. On the way to work.

Lance was up in a second, and I was shocked and happy to see him. "I thought you said that something came up," I said as I walked over to him.

"Yes, I got pulled into something, but I'm here." He gave me a tight squeeze, lifting me off my feet, and I could hear the growl coming from Atticus.

Chapter 14

When Lance released me, I looked around his arm to see Micah keeping Atticus in his seat.

My brother-in-law winked at me. All the other guys stood and gave me brief hugs, which again made Atticus growl. When I gave Micah a tight hug and he kissed me on top of my head, Atticus was less growly, but he muttered under his breath, "Do you have to touch her?"

Micah just chuckled. And then when I reached my husband, he dragged me onto his lap. "Ah, that's better."

"Atticus, baby, I can't sit on your lap while you guys are having... I don't know, what is this? A boys' meeting?"

"I'm just getting an update on everything."

"I would argue about how come I wasn't called in for an update as well, but we have bigger fish to fry right now."

My favorite smile disappeared. "What do you mean?" he asked gruffly.

"It's Morgan. She texted me. Remember that guy she was talking about the other day when you brought me home?"

Atticus's brow furrowed as he tried to process the information. "What guy? She didn't mention a guy."

Lance got very interested at that moment. "What guy? Morgan? She doesn't have any guys. Who could stand her for longer than ten minutes?"

I rolled my eyes. "It's the guy that my dad introduced her to."

Interestingly, it was Micah who remembered him. "Yeah,

the one who had a clingy had-to-keep-calling problem. I have a workup on him."

"Right. Well, I don't think we need a workup, but he is at the lounge, club, or wherever Morgan is, and he's creeping her out. So I'm going to—"

Before I could even say anything else, Atticus was standing with me in his arms. He planted me gently on my feet. "Micah, watch her. I'm going to get Morgan."

I blinked rapidly. "No, you don't have to do that. I was just coming to tell you that I was going to get her. Yes, I will take the bodyguards, and yes, I will be careful, but I just need to go and get my sister."

He gave me a look that I didn't enjoy being on the receiving end of. It was cold and icy. And well, pissed off.

No, that wasn't pissed off. That was... hurt? But why was he hurt?

"She's my sister too now, so I'm going to get her and keep you safe at the same time. I'm not going to invite trouble we don't need. So please, do me a favor. Stay here."

The other lads stood up.

"Atticus, she's not going to appreciate a hoard of hot men walking in to ruin her evening. Be reasonable."

Gavin grinned at me. "So, you think I'm hot."

Atticus sliced him a look so cold that Gavin stepped back and put his hands up. "Just kidding, man. Just kidding."

Lance rolled his shoulders. "I'm going with you."

Chapter 14

I laughed. "Lance, don't go with him. That's crazy. Besides, you can't save Morgan. That will *really* piss her off."

He then gave me a similar look to Atticus's. But this one held more pain. "I might think she's a pain in the ass, but she's kind of *my* pain in the ass, so if someone is bothering her, we need to fix it."

"Okay, fine, you two can go, but be discreet for fuck's sake. She won't like it. She'll be embarrassed. I just want her to know she has back up, okay? Lance, don't let Atticus do anything insane."

Lance just shrugged.

My husband reached out and kissed me on the temple. "Why didn't you ask me to go get her?"

"What? Isn't that what I just did?"

He shook his head. "No, you came to tell me that *you* were going. And then you acted like she wasn't my family too."

His voice was so low the others couldn't hear it. They were already dispersing, quickly taking assignments of what they were going to do next about trying to find whoever the hell was trying to kill me.

"Atticus, I—" But he was gone already with Lance on his heels. I glanced at my brother-in-law, who gave me a weak smile.

"He was just grumpy. Look, we didn't exactly have the best dad, as you know. Atticus has to feel like he's saving everyone. You know that. He will *always* volunteer, but he wants you to feel like you can ask, I guess. It's the better way to say that."

I sighed. "I just didn't think about it. I'm used to solving my own problems."

"Well, now you don't have to. You have six very good-looking men who are eager to do your bidding."

He gave me a little bow, and I laughed. "You lose the effect of saying *very good-looking*, if he's not here to hear it."

Micah winked. "Hey, I have to boost my own ego somehow."

"Right. So when he gets home, I'll fix it."

"I think it'll be a pretty easy fix. He loves you."

"Yeah, I know. I just hope that whatever is going on at the club isn't too serious. The last thing I want is for Atticus to get hurt."

"Really?" Micah laughed but then sobered quickly. "The thing you should probably worry about is Atticus hurting someone else. Especially if he thinks his family is under threat. He would do anything to protect you and your sister."

15

ATTICUS

We took the Maybach. And as the tires slid over the rain-slick streets, I slid a glance over at Lakewood. "So, you want to tell me why you're coming with me to get Morgan?"

He didn't even look at me. "She's like my sister. Why wouldn't I come if some creep is all over her?"

"No, I mean, that's why *I'm* going. But are you sure that's why you're going?"

He turned to me at that point. "Excuse me, weren't you the one insisting I was in love with your wife?"

I shrugged nonchalantly. "I think you were. Or at least *thought* you were. I don't blame you either. Gwen is gorgeous. And too kind for her own good. Not to mention brilliant. She keeps me on my toes, and she is funny without trying to be. So yeah, of course, I assume everyone is in love with her. Except, I think a part of you, maybe, is in love with the *idea* of her, but that's because you have a soft spot for her. And you *do* love her; you're just not *in love* with her, and I didn't see it until now."

He narrowed his gaze at me. "What the fuck are you talking about?"

I chuckled low under my breath. "Right, I'm not talking about anything. I am relieved that you're not in love with Gwen. And you should be relieved too. It makes me hate you less."

"I don't give a fuck if you hate me."

"Sure, you do. I am your boss."

"Well, technically, Gwen is my boss. And now she's your boss too, so..." He let his voice trail.

He had a point about that. Given that she had majority shares in my company, she could fire me at will. So I supposed she was my boss.

"Okay, fair point. But I do control your movement, so you still want me on your good side. And I like you now. Well, *like* is a strong word. But you get the idea."

"Morgan is also a kid, you know that, right?" he asked.

I sucked in a slow steady breath. "She is young. She's eighteen and needs to see the world a little. Maybe in a couple of years, but if I at all thought you were a creep, I'd be beating your ass."

"I'm not into Morgan."

I opted to let it go then. Far be it from me to tell the man

Chapter 15

what he wanted. He'd see it eventually. And then I would get the satisfaction of saying *I told you so.*

I pulled up to the club and tossed the valet my keys and a fresh bill from my wallet. The bouncer looked like he might try to dissuade us, but the hostess came running immediately and whispered something in his ear, and then he moved aside the velvet rope for us. Because of course he would.

When I spotted Morgan, I immediately noticed some asshole had her pinned at the bar, both hands on either side of her.

Hell, I didn't even get the chance to say shit before Lance was on the move.

"Lakewood, come the fuck—"

Lance didn't hear a word. He just peeled the idiot off and dragged him by the collar far the hell away from Morgan. He was taking him toward the back. I took Morgan's hand, and we had no choice but to follow.

Behind me, Morgan squeaked, "What the fuck? Where did you guys come from?"

"Your sister filled us in."

"Gwen?"

"Yeah, you have another sister?" I asked loudly over the din of the music.

"She worries too much. I thought she would just come."

"Well..." I pulled her past the throng of people waiting for the bathrooms. "You're her sister, so now you're my sister, and I need to protect you both. So it's me."

She blinked rapidly, her dark eyes welling up with tears. "Um, thanks. He wouldn't take no for an answer. And Atticus—"

I could see her getting more agitated by the second.

"H-he knows where I live. And he said—" She dragged in a quick, sharp breath. "He said that I could play hard-to-get all I wanted, but he knew where I lived and he would come and see me."

Fuck. Fuck. Fuck. "Well, he can try and see you all he wants, but you'll find that Park Tower is heavily guarded, and he won't make it past the lobby."

"Fuck, I don't live there. I live in the dorm."

"Not anymore, you don't."

Outside, Lance had the piece of shit up against the wall with his arm across his neck. The other guy took a swing, which Lance ducked easily.

"Goddamn it, Lance, let him go," Morgan cried. "You're only going to get yourself hurt."

I had to drag Morgan back because she was trying to jump into the fray. Lance ignored her.

"Lakewood, that's enough."

"Oh, is that what you said when you found out about Bronson?" He released the guy. Then the kid tried to take a swipe at him, and Lakewood landed an uppercut that snapped his jaws together and cocked his head back like a fucking Pez dispenser.

Chapter 15

I couldn't help it. My brows lifted, and I sucked in a short breath, because I knew that was going to hurt.

The dipshit stumbled and tried to brace himself against the wall, but Lance was behind him and put him in a chokehold as he growled low in his ear. "If I ever find you near her again, I swear to God, I will fucking kill you."

Beside me, Morgan sucked in a sharp gasp. I knew Gwen would be pissed if I let Lakewood kill someone. "Lakewood, ease up. We're not killing anyone today. It's a messy clean-up job. And then we have to worry about, you know, alibis and all that bullshit. I also don't know where the security camera is around here. So, you know, let's leave the murdering to another dark alley later where there are likely no cameras, okay?"

Next to me, Morgan breathed out his name. "Lance."

And his gaze skittered up, meeting hers.

She was the one who got through to him, and he slowly eased up on the guy's neck as dipshit sank to the ground, gasping for breath.

He gazed at Morgan, and I could see the obsession there. But then his gaze skittered to mine, which gave me a sense of satisfaction that he was aware of his surroundings again. And I hadn't even had to use my fists.

"You heard what he said, dipshit. He'll kill you. I, on the other hand, won't kill you if I see you again. I'll bury you somewhere, chained, and starving probably, and slowly torture you like the cruel sadistic bastard I am." I inclined my head to Lakewood. "Him, he's the nice one. He doesn't even like her, and that's what he's willing to do to you. Know that he's dead serious. To me, she's fucking family. If you come after her, you will pay. Not only with your life, but with your livelihood and your soul. She is mine to protect. Are we clear?"

He narrowed his gaze at me and then looked back to Morgan, but Lance stopped in his line of sight. "No, asshole, you don't even look at her. You look at him. When he's finished ruining your life, you'll be begging for me to end it."

And then dipshit began scooting backward, jumped to his feet, and ran.

When I was sure he'd kept running, I turned to Morgan. "Are you okay, kid?"

She had her arms wrapped around her. "He's a psychopath. He'll come back, won't he?"

I wanted to tell her no. I wanted to tell her that we'd keep her safe, but I knew that wasn't the case. For now, she needed to *feel* safe. And then I would figure out a long-term plan for dipshit. "Look, for now, let's get you home to the penthouse. You'll spend the night. It'll give your sister peace of mind, so she'll actually sleep, and in the morning, we'll take you to the police station and file a report. A restraining order should do the trick. I will have Pierce and Micah deal with your tech. New number, new email, all that stuff. Okay?"

She nodded slowly, her eyes skittering back to Lance.

Chapter 15

I turned to find him standing like a statuary, glowering into the darkness of the alley as if waiting for more trouble to come. "Lakewood, she's all right. Let's go."

He didn't turn to look at Morgan, but when he spoke, I knew he was talking to her. "Next time you see him, don't call your sister. You call me, do you understand?"

His voice was a low growl, and I swore I had never heard Lakewood sound like that *ever* about Gwen. He might not realize that he was into Morgan, which would be peace of mind for me and probably Gwen, but he was. And at some point, that was going to bubble over, and it was going to be messy, considering their volatility.

Her voice trembled. "Yeah, okay, I understand."

It was only then that he turned around to face us. It was almost like he'd put the mask back on. That even-keeled, easy-going version of Lance Lakewood was back. But I could see now that wasn't really Lance. The *real* him was just underneath with barely concealed rage and something else that ran deep. He would protect Morgan with his life. And maybe even more fiercely than he'd protected Gwen when I sent her to him. Maybe I had underestimated him after all.

"Come on, Morgan, let's go," I said, putting an arm around her shoulders. "And if you're good, I'll let you think of all the ways that we could ruin dipshit's life."

16

ATTICUS

After we dropped Lakewood off, I led Morgan through the lobby of the Park Tower, watching her carefully. "Are you okay?" I asked.

"You can stop asking me that."

"I know. I just figured maybe it was scary. Do you like, want to talk or something?"

My sister-in-law laughed. "What? We're going to become besties now, are we, Atticus?"

I shrugged as I pushed the elevator button. "I don't know. Maybe."

She eyed me warily. "I guess I just feel stupid. And God, I really hate the fact that Lance saw me like that."

"Lance didn't see you like anything. He saw some guy overstepping, and he acted like any good guy would."

"Yeah, but he is Gwen's best friend. He has seen me do

Chapter 16

some stupid teenage shit. Like once, I went to a friend's party and maybe, just maybe, over indulged on the alcohol. I needed Gwen to come rescue me, which was embarrassing to say the least."

"She's your sister. She loves you."

"Yeah, but she brought Lance. And well, you can imagine. Lance thought I was the biggest idiot he'd ever seen." We stepped in the elevator and she leaned against the back wall as she talked.

"You know, I don't think you see Lance as clearly as you think you do."

"Oh, I see him and all his judgment. He acts like he was never young. Except Gwen has shown me the pictures of his blitzed-out drunk days. And how do you even get drunk like that? Anyway, he's like a very judgy big brother."

I nodded. "Right, big brother."

"He's always in my shit."

"Well, I can promise that I will not always be in your shit unless I think you're going to get yourself hurt. And then, well, I might get brotherly."

She grinned at me. "You know, I've said it before, but I think you're actually really good for Gwen."

I gave her a look of surprise. "Well, you've never said it to me before, so thanks, I guess."

"And she's good for you too. She makes you more, I don't know, human?"

"At least there is that."

She shrugged. "Well, you're a bit stiff."

I rolled my eyes. "Wow, tell me how you really feel."

"You're like a hot robot."

"Ooouch." I clutched my heart, acting wounded. But she was right, obviously. "Damn, I have to remember to keep my wits around the Becker girls."

"Nah, Gwen is all googly-eyed about you. She'd never hurt your feelings and call you a robot to your face."

"Oh yes, she has. But she had a point. She wanted me to *feel* my feelings."

Morgan grinned. "And did you tell her to feel her feelings too?"

"You know what's interesting? She was less inclined to do so than I was."

"Yeah well, we haven't exactly been taught that feeling our feelings is a safe space. But in the interest of making my therapist happy, thank you for coming to get me. I was scared."

I gave her a soft smile. "That's fair. And if I were you, I would have been scared too. Sorry if we came off a little heavy-handed."

"No, you were great. Lance was the heavy-handed one. You don't actually think he would kill him, do you?"

I watched her closely for a moment. She really had no idea. *Okay then, this is going to be entertaining to watch over the next several years.* "Probably not on purpose." It's not how Lakewood rolled. But truth be told, I had also

Chapter 16

underestimated him. So I didn't think he would have murder-murdered him, but accidental murder? Sure. It was possible.

"Wow, he really needs some anger management classes."

I choked on a laugh.

"What's so funny?" she asked.

I studied her. She was smart, but Lakewood was right. She was a kid. She didn't see it. "The way you two dance around each other is funny."

"We do not dance around each other. He's a pain in the ass. And who assigned him as my big brother anyway? Because I don't need a big brother."

I grinned at her. "Well, you have one now."

"You don't count. You don't know me nearly as well as he does. Sometimes I just want to put a fist to his face."

I assessed her. "Do you even know how to make a fist?"

"How hard can it be? Men do it all the time."

I winced at that. "I hope that is something you do not practice. However, if you want to learn, I can have one of the boys start working with you on self-defense."

Her eyes went wide. "Oh, like Krav Maga and shit?"

"Yes, I have a trainer. It's actually not the worst idea in the world for you and Gwen to get some basic self-defense training."

"Oh my God, yes. Dad would never let us do anything like that. He said that we were girls, so we should be ladylike. I don't know what he thought was going to happen, but I guess he didn't want us to be seen as angry black females, so he really prided himself on instilling extra femininity."

"That is so bullshit."

"Well, he wasn't entirely wrong, but he's also not entirely right."

What the hell did I know? And why had I never asked Gwen about any of this?

"Okay, in that case, let me be a good big brother. Would you *like* to learn?"

"How to take care of myself? Yeah. I guess I wouldn't feel so helpless, like having to call my big sister to come and rescue me."

I nodded. "Okay, that is something I can definitely help to take care of."

"You're serious? You'll teach me?"

"Um, not me personally, but yeah, we can figure something out."

"Oh my God, that is actually really cool of you."

The elevator reached the top floor, and I got my eyes scanned to open the doors. When asked for additional identification due to the weight of the elevator, I had Morgan come over for a thumbprint. "Well, it's a little late," I said, "so I don't know if Gwen is still up. But you know where the guest room is, right?"

"You mean one of the five?"

"Yes. Just pick one. Micah is in one of them, so you might

Chapter 16

want to knock before you walk in because God only knows what he might be doing in there."

She hesitated in the foyer as I dropped my keys in the bowl. "Um, I know I said it before, but thanks and shit."

"Of course. And Morgan, I meant it when I said I would like us to be closer. Not just for Gwen, but for me. I feel like I could learn a lot from you."

Her grin was so reminiscent of Gwen's, and it lit up her entire face. Dual dimples peeking out, making you instantly feel warm inside. I was going to have to lock her up in here. The guys were going to be knocking on the door, and I would definitely need to add more security, but it would need to be discreet. Because even more than Gwen, Morgan needed freedom. She needed to be as free as possible to figure out who the hell she was going to be, and she couldn't do that with a close watch.

"Now you're giving me a worried look. What's that all about?" she asked playfully.

"Nothing. It's just that I've only had a baby brother. I mostly just played swords with him, so I want to know what to do with a sister. You'll need to teach me that, too."

"Oh my God, it's going to be awesome," she said with a laugh. "Let me paint your toenails."

I shook my head. "I regret this already."

"I'm just fucking with you. But we're going to do some little sister-big brother activities. We're going to pick one weekend a month where you do everything I'd say."

"Yep, I'm *really* going to regret this," I muttered.

"No, you won't. It will make you more *human*. Besides, it'll be stuff that you can deal with. We'll include Gwen too. It will help you open up your mind. Hell, you should totally join Micah's romance novel reading club. I mean it. The one we're reading right now is a hacking romance where the girl is also a vampire."

My brows lifted. "Wait, she's a hacker *and* a vampire? Is her love interest a vampire too?"

She rolled her eyes at me like I was a moron, because honestly, this couldn't be real. "No, he's a werewolf of course, hello."

Oh my God. How did I get out of this conversation?

She pumped her eyebrows. "Think of it as urban fantasy with lots of spice."

I swallowed hard. None of this made any sense. "You know what, I don't want to know about you reading spice. What the hell has Micah got you reading?"

"Oh please, I was reading these books long before he was. And I recommended this book to him."

The way her eyes danced, I knew she was deadly serious. "You know what? It's bedtime. Down the hall that way, every bedroom has a bathroom, and there are always spare toothbrushes and toothpaste and a couple of different sets of pajamas in the closet."

But I didn't need to direct her anywhere because Gwen was lying on the couch, and the moment she heard the sound of Morgan's shoes on the floor, she sat up. "Oh, there you guys are. Morgan, are you okay?"

Morgan nodded and then went over and gave her sister a raspberry on the cheek. "I'm fine. Atticus and Lance came to get me."

Gwen glanced around the two of us. "Where's Lance?"

"We dropped him off at home."

"Home? Is he at a hotel or something?" she asked, obviously confused.

I shook my head. "No, he kept his apartment. I guess he assumed he might be back."

"Right. But I thought he'd rented it out."

"I guess not. Anyway, we're back. Morgan is going to be staying here for a while."

Gwen blinked at me rapidly. "How long is a while?"

Morgan exchanged a glance with me. "Um, Atticus was saying that maybe I should stay here so you guys could keep an eye on me. Keep me out of trouble."

I could see what she was doing. But I let her do it. "Yeah, I figured you'd be happier if she was here. And the subway goes straight down to NYU. She doesn't need to stay in the dorm."

"Yeah, no sharing showers," Morgan said with a giggle. "I'd planned to move off campus anyway, but if I can stay here with the sauna and the massage room, then why not do that?"

Gwen just laughed. "Well, it'll be great to have you here.

It's not like we don't have room." She just looked so at peace and happy. I wanted her to look like that all the time.

Morgan came back over and launched herself at me, and I had to think fast and catch her quick. She leaned up, clearly expecting me to bend down. And when I did, she gave me a raspberry. A wet, slobbery raspberry. Then she jumped down and gave me a wink. "Thanks, big bro. I appreciate the rescue."

Before I knew it, she was skipping off to a guest room. She picked the one next to Micah, because apparently, she was going to Morse Code him some of the pages of the books they were reading so that he could hurry up and get to the good part.

Whatever that meant.

When I turned my gaze to my wife, she had tears in her eyes. "You invited her to come live with us?"

I shrugged. "For as long or as little as she wants. I didn't know how you were going to feel about that, but I figured it would make you happy. You love having her around. You worry about her. It's cool. And this way, you can keep an eye on her comings and goings."

"How bad was it?" Her voice was soft when she asked.

"Nothing I couldn't handle. And Morgan was handling it pretty great herself. Surprisingly, it was Lance who didn't handle it well. He threatened to kill the guy."

Gwen winced and sat up straighter. "Oh, shit. That doesn't sound like Lance."

Chapter 16

"It's fine. I didn't let him kill anyone."

"Well, I appreciate that, because had it been you, you might have killed him."

"Lance seems very protective of your little sister."

Her gaze landed on mine and held. "So, you're thinking what I'm thinking?"

I shrugged. "Yeah, I'm thinking he has a thing for her. He feels weird about it because she's still so young."

"I feel a little weird about it too, but it's like a tangible thing in the air. Like when they're in the room together, you can feel that crackle. I don't think it's avoidable, but we'll stay out of it."

"Okay," I said, climbing over the back of the couch to join her after I took off my shoes.

She was smashed underneath me, and she giggled. "Atticus Price, we now have an impressionable young mind in the house. We need to be a little bit more careful."

"Well, do you even know what kind of dirty shit Micah and your sister are reading? There's a werewolf, and he's in love with a vampire. He plays hockey. I don't know what that has to do with anything, but apparently, there are spicy parts. And *she* recommended the book to *him*. Honestly, I am traumatized. If I had pearls, I would clutch them. I don't think either one of them is going to care, but I'm going to finger my wife on this couch right now."

Gwen's gasp was soft. "Who said you could finger me? You didn't let me go get my sister."

My hand reached under the blanket and traced up her thigh. She was wearing shorts. Apparently, she'd lost the sweatpants after I left and was back in those little shorts that hugged her ass just so.

"You know the words to say to make me stop."

She squirmed beneath me, lifting her hips, trying to guide my fingers where they already wanted to go.

"You don't need to do that, Ness; I know the way." I nuzzled her neck and nipped, finding her sweet pussy and tracing a thumb over her clit. "See? I told you I knew my way."

She groaned. "Atticus..."

"Say the word if you want me to stop."

"Morgan is going to catch us."

"I think your sister is smart enough to know that if you are on the couch and we're in the same room together, that she should make lots of noise before coming back out."

I waited for her to say no. But when she rolled her hips against my thumb again, my fingers dipped under her shorts and found her sweet pussy wet and slick.

"Fuck. I love how you're always ready for me."

"This is hardly fair," she muttered.

"Who said I was playing fair? Are you still mad at me?"

She bit her lip. "Maybe I'll just put a pin in my annoyance for now."

I nipped at her neck. "That's a very good idea, Ness." My thumb slid over her clit again. Fuck, all I wanted to do was

Chapter 16

slide her shorts off and sink into her on the couch. Damn whoever might see or hear anything.

Just the idea of my hand clamped over her mouth to keep her quiet while she came around my cock had me rocking my hips against her.

"You're using sex to speed up my forgiveness," she teased.

"Maybe, but you want to forgive me. I'm still going to make you come on my fingers and maybe my cock. Or maybe I'll just rub up against you like we would have in high school."

Her hips lifted then. "You know how I love a good dry humping. There's something so forbidden and sexy in it."

"Then dry humping it is. But first, come on my fingers."

"Okay, fine. I'm on my way to forgiving you. But you're going to have to give me many more orgasms first."

"Done deal. Now spread your thighs, baby. I want to make this good."

I slipped my hand further beneath the waistband of her shorts, my fingers making contact with the warm fevered flesh they sought. She gasped, a tiny jolt of surprise that quickly melted into a moan of anticipation. "Oh, Atticus, don't tease."

"Teasing's part of the game, love," I breathed back, my thumb circling her clit once more before dipping lower to enter her.

I kissed the skin of her neck, trailing my lips up to whisper in her ear.

"I love making you moan, Ness."

She groaned once more, pushing against my fingers. My digits were slick with desire as they slipped inside her, finding that sweet spot that always made her gasp and writhe beneath me. She was close already. I could tell by the hitch in her breath and the way she clung to my arm for support.

"Atticus," she whimpered, tipping her head back as I increased the pressure on her clit.

"Shhh," I murmured against her skin, the taste of her salty sweat sweet on my lips. "We wouldn't want your sister to hear, would we? Or worse, Micah." Nipping at her ear, I added. "Or is that what you want? For him to hear you?"

She whimpered again, biting her lip to silence herself. I nipped at her earlobe, my fingers sinking further into her warm depths. She was slick and hot around me, and the urge to replace my hand with something far more satisfying was nearly overwhelming.

Her body stiffened briefly underneath me, her grip on my shoulder tightening as she shook her head vehemently. "Oh, Atticus," she managed to whisper between gasps for air.

"Good," I murmured against her neck, my fingers moving inside her with a rhythm that we'd both come to know so well.

Her breath hitched again as I hit just the right spot. "Oh God, Atticus," she whimpered, her back arching off the couch.

Reaching down, I used my other hand to tug the waist-

Chapter 16

band of her shorts down enough to slide my fingers out and over the bare skin of her ass.

With a newfound vigor, I moved my fingers inside her once more, this time spreading them apart to touch her in just the right way.

"Atticus." Her voice was little more than a breathless whisper now as she gripped onto me tighter. "I-I'm going to..."

"Shhh," I chuckled into her ear, my lips brushing against the shell of it.

"Hold it, love. Hold on for just a bit longer." I coaxed her with my words while my thumb went back to work on her clit.

She writhed beneath me, whispering my name like a prayer as I pushed her closer and closer to the precipice of pleasure.

And then, she broke.

Her climax echoed through the room silently, save for the quiet whispers of our names escaping each other's lips. She trembled in my arms, sticky with sweat but glowing with satisfaction, my fingers still buried deep inside her.

17

GWEN

I couldn't move.

All I could do was lay there with one leg hooked over the back of the couch, my shorts dangling off one foot, my legs quivering, with Atticus's fingers buried in my pussy and one grazing my asshole.

"Oh my God. I think you broke me," I whispered.

Atticus kneeled between my thighs, his gaze locked onto how he had my lips spread, and he pumped his fingers into me again. "There's nothing fucking sexier than watching you squeeze around me, Ness."

He grinned at me wickedly, his fingers still deep inside me. His thumb circled my clit in a slow, torturous rhythm that had my breath hitching. My hand clutched at the back of the couch.

Chapter 17

"Atticus." I hissed his name as my body tensed, a fire spreading from my core and winding its way throughout my limbs. His fingers quickened their pace, pushing me closer to the edge.

Then he removed his fingers from me, putting them into his mouth and sucking on them while continuing to gaze down at me. The sight left me breathless and wanting more.

"Does my sweet pussy miss me already?" Atticus's voice was pure gravel as he spoke. His movements were jerky as he yanked out his belt then unzipped his jeans.

"Yes," I whimpered, my responding shiver apparently the answer he was seeking. His hands moved to his waistband, pulling the fabric down to reveal his hard length. I gasped at the sight, my gaze locked onto him.

A devilish grin spread across his face, and he grazed his thumb over my clit once more for good measure. "You're gonna feel how much I've missed you."

With that, he positioned himself at my entrance, his length teasing my swollen lips. My breath hitched in anticipation as he leaned in, his mouth crashing onto mine in a fierce kiss before he slid his length against me.

"Ah, fuck..." His voice was rough, strained as he slid against me. Every inch of him slid against my pussy, making me cry out at the sweet sensation. Slowly, he began to move in long deep strokes that sent waves of pleasure cascading through me.

"Is this what we would have done if I'd known you as a teenager?" he whispered. "Would I have snuck into your room?"

Oh God, his words had me lifting my hips. "God, I need this."

His teeth nipped my neck as he rubbed against me, his cock sliding through my folds. "You were a good girl then, weren't you? You would have wanted to stay a virgin. But maybe I could have tempted you to get close." He groaned against my lips.

The grind of his hips and his words were exquisite. He shoved his hands in my hair and tugged, angling my neck back. Then he delved his tongue inside my mouth as my nails dug into his shoulders.

His words, his touches, everything he was doing to me was driving me insane. I could feel every nerve in my body singing for him, begging for more. My hands flew up his back, clawing at the fabric of his shirt. He groaned against my mouth, a sound that shot straight to my core.

"I would have passed every test just to be with you," I confessed between breaths. My voice came out shaky and desperate, matching the trembling desire coursing through my body. "Even if it wasn't... all the way."

His breath hitched at my words, his rhythm faltering for a moment before he pushed harder against me, earning a moan from both of us. "Jesus, Ness," he murmured into my ear. "We would've been unstoppable."

Chapter 17

I laughed breathlessly at that. "We could've set the world on fire. There is no way just feeling you against me would have been enough."

"Never enough. Fuck, you would have had me on my knees just at the hope of my dick touching your softness." He chuckled against my earlobe before nipping at it gently. His thrusts grew more desperate, more passionate, as if each word that left my mouth spurred him on further.

"I would have memorized every inch of your body, Ness," he confessed raggedly, his entire body shuddering against mine. The desperation in his voice was mirrored by the frantic rhythm he set, our bodies rocking together on the couch.

"Yeah, yeah, Atticus," I gasped out, my nails digging into his back as I clung to him. His thrusts were relentless, driving me closer and closer to the brink of ecstasy.

"And you would have driven me insane," he continued breathlessly. "With your teasing and sultry smiles. I would have been hard for you every damn day." His teeth grazed my exposed collarbone, drawing a shaky moan from my lips.

Reaching between us, he pushed his cock down to tease my entrance, shifting his weight so every slide of his cock threatened to finally penetrate. "We would have said it was only teasing and we weren't going to fuck, but then naughty little thing that you are, you would have started begging for just the tip," he murmured as he dragged the head of his cock over my entrance then kissed me thoroughly.

At his words, a whimper strangled itself in my throat. His every word, the weight of each syllable, was plunging me lower into a trance. It was as if we were not here and now, but back then... teenagers sneaking around, risking everything for a taste of forbidden fruit.

His thumb moved to rub my clit again, making my hips jerk upward. My body was screaming for friction, demanding more than just words and touches and teases.

"I would have," I confessed breathlessly. "I would have been begging for you."

A moan escaped Atticus at the sound of my words echoing back his own fantasies. He slid himself against me again, just skimming my entrance but not penetrating. He relished torturing me with the imminent promise of release.

"Damn, Ness," he muttered, his hot breath fanning on my neck. His thrusts grew erratic, an indication that he was nearing the edge too.

"I would have done anything to feel you inside me," I said, my voice barely above a whisper now. Even though we were reminiscing about what could have been, it felt intimate and raw and real.

At that, Atticus let out a low growl. "Fuck, baby, I want to come so bad, but I'm not going without you."

His hand slid down to where his cock rubbed over my clit. His touch was masterful, evoking a moan that tore from my throat. "Atticus..." I whispered. My voice was hoarse, filled with the raw need that his words and touch had ignited. His thumb took over, dragging me to the edge of oblivion by force as he stroked his dick with his other hand.

I clutched his forearms for support as he grinned devilishly down at me. When my orgasm snatched my soul, dragging me over the edge, I stiffened, arching my back, a silent scream on my lips.

All I could do was watch in awe as Atticus stroked himself from root to tip above me, his lips parted, harsh pants escaping as his eyes stayed glued on my pussy.

His hand moved faster as his gaze remained fixated on my body. His body was tight, the cords of muscle in his arm working rhythmically. I could hear the erratic gasps escaping his lips, and I knew he was hanging on by a thread.

His strokes quickened, every slide of his hand accompanied by a fervent groan that echoed through the quiet room. I was still in the throes of my own orgasm, my body shaking with aftershocks, sensations heightened by the sight of him hovering over me.

"Look at me, Atticus. Give it to me."

The tension built once again, my body sinking into the soft cushions of our leather couch. His voice filled the room, desperation becoming more evident with every breath he took. "I'm... I'm..." he stuttered, his grip tightening on his hardness.

When Atticus came apart above me, his cry of release filled my ears while his body shuddered uncontrollably over mine.

Hot spurts painted my belly as he continued to stroke himself through the climax, watching as he painted my pussy and my belly in his cum.

Harsh breath still tearing out of him, he stroked two fingers over my pussy lips, then brought them to my lips to taste them. When I peeked my tongue out to lick his fingers, Atticus groaned through tightly clenched teeth. "Fuck, you're so goddamn pretty. I'm still hard. I'm not done. Can I, baby? Will you let me push my cock into you?"

Holy shit.

"Atticus," I moaned, my fingers delving into his hair. "Please..."

With a groan, he gave in, pushing his length inside me so slowly I felt every inch. A cry of pure bliss erupted from my throat as he finally seated himself deep within me, where I needed him the most.

"Fuck, Ness," Atticus cursed, his voice filled with awe and adoration as he began to move within me. The rhythm was slow and deliberate, every stroke designed to drive me wild with pleasure and anticipation.

His hands cradled my face as he moved above me, looking down into my eyes as he whispered sweet promises and sinful provocations that would have driven a high school girl absolutely mad with desire.

"We would've been dangerous together." His voice was low, hot against my flushed skin. "Driving each other crazy with need and desire. Temptation always just a touch away."

Chapter 17

"Always," I breathed out raggedly as his thrusts became more insistent. "I would have given anything just to feel you like this."

Atticus's lips crashed onto mine, capturing my response in a heated kiss. Our tongues mingled while his hand slid down my body in search of more. He cupped my breast, his fingers circling the hardened bud before giving it a firm squeeze. A loud moan escaped my lips at the action, and he chuckled into my mouth, the vibration sending shivers down my body.

"God, you're so fucking sexy," Atticus growled as he pulled away from our kiss only to attach his lips to the valley between my breasts. He gave each nipple equal attention before moving lower and sliding out of me, leaving a trail of open-mouthed kisses down my stomach.

His movements slowed when he reached the junction of my thighs, his eyes darting up to hold my gaze. His facial expression was hard to read at that moment. It was as if he was holding back a force that might rip him apart.

"Will you let me taste you?" he asked in a voice that barely reached above a whisper. I could feel him waiting for an answer, but I couldn't find the words. My mind was spinning and caught in the wave of desire that had consumed us both.

Instead, I nodded. I swallowed dryly, my mouth felt like sandpaper. The anticipation had been building up since we had fallen onto the sofa, and now it was almost painful.

Atticus wasted no time in fulfilling his promise, his tongue stroked over me with a newfound hunger. His eyes stayed trained on mine as he worked me over and over again with his mouth and fingers. Each stroke sent waves of pleasure coursing through my veins, every touch seemed to ignite a part of me that had been dormant for far too long.

The room filled with the sounds of our groans. I should care about what Morgan could hear, but I was too far gone. My breath hitched on every sensation, every slide of his tongue or push of his fingers brought me closer to the edge. His name slipped from my lips in a needy plea, and my hands tangled in his hair, holding him to me.

His tongue lapped at me faster, his fingers pumping into me in tandem with his mouth. I gasped and whimpered, my body arching off the couch as an orgasm rocked through me.

He was there, catching every moan and gasp, soothing me through the waves of pleasure until I was boneless beneath him. His kisses were soft then, trailing up my belly and breasts until he was kissing me again. His tongue played lazily with mine, and it tasted like the two of us combined.

"Mine," he murmured against my lips after breaking our kiss. There was something different in his eyes when he gazed down at me this time. A sense of finality that wasn't there before.

Before I could respond, Atticus thrust back into me with a force that had my breath hitching in surprise. His strokes

Chapter 17

were deliberate and hard, each one hitting a spot deep within me, making me see stars behind my closed eyelids.

"You're mine," he repeated again, like a mantra, his voice raw and filled with emotion. Every thrust included the words *you're mine* like an oath or pledge of his love. He claimed me over and over again until I surrendered to him completely.

And then he finally collapsed above me, spent.

18

GWEN

Two days after Atticus brought my sister home, he still hadn't let up on the overprotective bit. Nope. My husband pinned me with a serious stare. "You're to stay here, Gwen."

I frowned as the car squeezed into a tight spot at a warehouse in the meat packing district.

"Oh my God, haven't you gotten your need to be overbearing out of your system for the day? You have a sister-in-law to smother now. Why do I need to stay here? What's the worst that could happen? Besides, there's a boutique down the way. I could just go and pop in there."

"Sven, stay with her."

"Yes, sir."

I rolled my eyes. "Oh my God, if you weren't going to let me do anything, then what is the point in bringing me along?"

Chapter 18

"You're doing something adjacent."

I narrowed my gaze. "Haven't we already had the discussion about how you're supposed to include me in the plans?"

"Yes, we have. And I'm including you. See, you're here, aren't you? I didn't sneak out to do this on my own."

I whacked him on the shoulder. The man did not budge, though he did give me the stupid dimples, which meant, 'Oh, God, aren't you cute?'

"But you're not letting me *do* anything."

"It's better if you don't. But this way, at least you get to hear about it right away. On the ground, so to speak."

"I swear to God, I can murder you when you're asleep, you know."

"I am aware. You literally hold my dick in your hands. Constantly," he reminded me. "However, you haven't started your self-defense training yet, so in case things get wild and crazy, I want to be the one who handles it."

"Atticus, you won't have a bodyguard with you if Sven stays with me."

"Yes, well, you're more likely to get in trouble than I am."

I scowled and watched as he strode toward the run-down apartment building. It was wedged between two warehouses, and it looked like one of those buildings where the landlord refused to give the property up to developers while all around it the neighborhood was changing. I could remember when the meatpacking district had been exactly what it sounded like.

It had been one area of town where my father had forbidden us from going when we were kids. But then somewhere along the way, it changed. Much like everything else. Thanks to gentrification, fashion houses, and avant-garde artists, everything changes eventually.

Atticus looked handsome as hell. He was wearing his peacoat, as there was a chill in the air today. I knew for a fact that would eventually come off, leaving him in a vest. All I wanted to do was peel his clothes off and lick him.

You can do that later. At home.

Since we'd almost gotten caught by his assistant, Andrew, *again*, we'd had to institute a new rule. No more fucking in the office. At least not unless it was behind closed and *locked* doors.

When Atticus left the car, that cute ass climbing up the stairs with a purpose, I sighed in the seat. "Sven, I know you're not going to let me in the building, but can I at least get out of the car?"

Sven frowned, his slight Norwegian accent crisp and clear. "No, Miss. Not wise."

And then a thought occurred to me. "Sven, you're an employee of Pendragon, right? Or does Atticus employ you personally?"

"Technically, ma'am, I am an employee of Pendragon."

"Oh, that's excellent," I said cheerfully. "So technically, *I'm* your boss."

Chapter 18

I watched as his brow furrowed. "Well, I suppose since you are the majority shareholder. But that does not mean—"

I was out of the car in seconds.

"Mrs. Price, please get back in the car."

"I swear to God, I told you, Sven, call me Gwen."

"Gwen, get in the car," he muttered.

"Now would you tell Atticus that, too?"

"If it's a safety concern, yes. I am technically under Mr. Trent's supervision. So I am really here for security."

"Ah, Pierce works for me, too. Isn't that great?"

"Ma'am, please." His sigh was exasperated.

"Oh. My. God." I rounded on him and stuck my finger in his chest. "If you call me ma'am one more time, I swear to God, I'll deck you on the spot."

"Sorry, Gwen. It's your safety, and I don't think Mr. Price would like you getting out of the car."

"I know he won't like it, but he's gone to talk to the kid. And if I know kids, even if he's not in trouble, he's going to run. So let's go."

"But Mr. Price said—"

"Yes, I know what he said. I also know he's gone to the front. And the kid won't go that way when he runs. So come with me."

He sighed. "Mrs. Price."

"Hey, at least I didn't open the door and start running," I reasoned.

"I'd be compelled at that point to run after you."

"God, you're so stodgy."

Sven nodded. "If you say so."

"I do. Now please, relax."

With Sven acting as my shadow basically, we went around the back of the building, through the alley, and I could sense his discomfort. "What's the problem, Sven? No one knows we're back here. No one is going to shoot at me. I promise."

"You are vulnerable. Mr. Price won't like that."

"I promise it's okay. Besides, Atticus can't tell me what to do."

I watched the muscle in his jaw tick as if he wanted to argue but wasn't going to bother.

And sure enough, as I'd predicted, the back door swung open and out came the kid, running full tilt. He was so busy looking behind him for Atticus that he didn't see me.

Unfortunately for him, Sven stepped directly in front of him, meaning to stop him from running into me, and effectively clotheslined him.

Atticus came running out the back door behind him, startled when he saw the two of us, and tripped over a garbage can.

Sven had the kid, but he wiggled out of his jacket, coming straight for me. And as he attempted to maul through me like a defensive line, I stuck out my foot and tripped him.

He went down hard on the asphalt, and I lowered myself next to him. "You must be Philip Mangles. Listen, all we

Chapter 18

want to do is talk. There's no need to run and get my husband and the bodyguard all upset. I'm Gwen. Do you mind if I ask you a couple of questions?"

Atticus looked irritated.

Sven looked like he would rather be anywhere but there. And the kid looked like he wanted to throw up as he darted glances between Sven, myself, and Atticus.

"Don't worry about them. The big Viking is paid to look annoyed. And my husband... that's just his normal face."

I could tell in the twitch of Atticus's nose that he was tempted to laugh, but he was perhaps too irritated with me in the moment. As for Sven, he was just maintaining his Viking composure.

"What do you want with me?" The kid fidgeted, and I could tell he did not want to be seen with us. Or he was tweaking. Maybe both.

"Look, a few weeks ago there was a shooting in front of the Park Tower."

His face paled. "I had nothing to do with that. It wasn't me. I-I don't even know how to shoot. I've never held a gun."

Sven stepped forward, and I planted my hand on his chest. The big Swede stopped, but I doubt it was because I was strong. It was because my husband was growling next to him.

"Both of you, shut it." I turned back to the kid. "You're not in trouble. No one thinks you shot anyone. Technically, me." I indicated my shoulder. "I took a bullet."

The kid's eyes widened in what could only be described as awe. "I didn't shoot you."

"I know that. But I think you saw who did."

"Look, I don't know nothin' about nothin'. I just want to go home. I just want to be left alone."

This time, Atticus did step forward. "Tell my wife what she wants to know."

That little shiver that always skipped down my spine when he said 'my wife' did its thing, and I thought it was a very inappropriate time for his voice to be doing those things to me.

"My husband is just very particular about me getting shot. Just tell us what you know."

The kid shifted his gaze to Sven, avoiding eye contact with Atticus, who was inching closer the more he looked at me. "I-I've seen him around town. He climbed into a car after looking at the building and then headed down the street. Later I saw him hanging around the lobby of an office building nearby. I always notice when he's there because I go to the doughnut shop to see this girl I want to ask out."

Atticus gave him a steady-eyed glower that said, *Get on with it.*

"That lobby is crazy busy. Everyone is in suits and stuff, you know? So that guy stood out. He just sat quietly in the window, staring at the building across the street. I saw him again two weeks later. Never thought anything of it. Even

Chapter 18

the night of the shooting, I didn't know he was up to no good."

Atticus's voice was low and full of gravel. "What were you doing there?"

The kid shrugged. "I sometimes go up in the building, you know? Like me and my friends would just go and fuck around there, smoke and shit."

Before Atticus could throttle the kid, I stepped in. "You're not in trouble. We just need you to tell us what you know."

The kid swallowed hard. "Anyway, he approached me and asked if I knew a way in this building. He gave me a hundred bucks, so I showed him."

My heart hammered in my chest. "Did you get a good look at him? Like really good? You've seen him in the light, right?"

The kid blinked rapidly, a small frown marring his forehead as if he just realized the man he'd told us about was dangerous. "But like, if you're telling me he's the shooter, then he knows my face too."

"He won't come for you. He's not looking for you. He is looking for me," I whispered.

"Shit. I never should have narced." He tried to wiggle out of my hold. He swallowed hard as he glanced at Atticus who growled low. "Let me go. I saw nothing."

"*I've* seen your face, and I promise you I am far more dangerous than that shooter."

The kid's Adam's apple bobbed up and down, and his pupils were pin pricks in his blue-gray eyes. "Yeah, of course... I did see him. But it's not like I have a picture or anything. Can't you get his image off the camera? In the coffeeshop across the street from the building?"

The kid had a point. We didn't know who we were looking for.

Atticus nodded. "We're done here."

Sven held the kid's jacket out to him as if we'd been having a very lovely exchange and now he was leaving.

"Thank you for your time," I said. "I appreciate it."

He blinked at me owlishly. "That's it?"

"Yeah, that's it."

"And you're not going to tell him about me, right?"

I shook my head. "No. But maybe stay close to the garage for the next few weeks. And stay out of trouble, okay? No more going back to the building. I don't want him to find you there."

"Sure. Um, thanks."

I shrugged. "Of course."

The kid took off running down the alley and then out into the street. As soon as he was gone, Atticus turned to me. "Just what the fuck are you doing out here?"

I crossed my arms and lifted my chin. "I actually got information out of the kid. Your wonder twin over here would have scared him half to death."

"That's the point. That's *how* you get information."

Chapter 18

"There's more than one way to skin a cat. And you catch a lot more flies with honey than with vinegar."

He rolled his eyes. "Are you done with the clichés? I gave you strict instructions to stay in the car."

I fixed a sassy smirk on my face. "You're going to have to realize, Atticus Price, that sometimes you need the backup. He came running out. If we hadn't been here, he might have made it to the street, and then you would have lost him."

"No, I wouldn't have."

"Okay, whatever you say."

"I gave you instructions to stay in the car," he repeated.

"Well..." I tilted my chin up at him, giving him a sassy smirk. "There's one thing you should remember, Atticus Price; I do not work for you."

19

GWEN

I WAS LATE. I only had thirty minutes to get dressed and ready. Atticus was meeting me at the restaurant. Of course, I'd gotten a little distracted at work, so that meant I had to hurry. Twenty-nine minutes now.

The photo recognition took a moment to activate, but then the doors finally slid open, and I ran in, tossing my keys in the bowl in the vestibule and jogging through the foyer before I realized I heard voices in the living room. When I rounded the corner, there was my sister, animatedly chatting with her hands, braids piled high on her head, a few curls hanging down in tendrils to frame her face. God, she looked like our mom. She was talking to a blond-haired woman who had her back turned to me. When Morgan saw me, she grinned.

"There you are. Remember how I said I was doing a

Chapter 19

paper on New York's oldest charities and the women behind them? I want you to meet Lucy Dexton."

And even though I was in a rush and moving at a rapid pace, the world slowed down as a very familiar woman turned around. Her smile was wide. It was Lucy. My husband's ex.

I stopped so abruptly that I wobbled in my heels and face-planted right over the back of the couch. I quickly righted myself. "Oh, um, hello again."

Morgan stood up, confusion written on her face. "This is my sister Gwen making the grand entrance. Gwen, this is Lucy."

"Um, yeah," I stuttered. "Actually, we've met. At my engagement party."

Morgan's brows lifted, and Lucy stood and said, "Hi, Gwen. It's good to see you again. I guess your sister didn't tell you I'd be coming."

I shook my head. "No, Morgan didn't mention it. But I didn't know she was interviewing people at the house."

I knew that the guys downstairs wouldn't let her pass if she didn't have clearance, so she must be safe, but when did that happen?

"Yeah, your sister and I have just been talking about charities and the different foundations I've been on. It's been a lovely chat. I understand that you and your sister were running Hearts and Hope. I'm so sorry to hear that the previous gala was the last of its kind. It was an institution that was so well attended over the last decade or so."

"Yeah, it's a shame. I'm so sorry, ladies, but I am in a hurry. I need to go meet Atticus. Um, Lucy, it was good to see you again." I said it through clenched teeth. I didn't mean it. I wanted to know what the fuck that woman was doing in my house.

I gave my sister a tight smile as I jogged into my bedroom, peeling off my jacket and trying to step out of my jeans as I hopped around.

Luckily, Magda had already prepared my dress. It had been steamed and pressed, and the white chiffon plunging neckline was perfect. I hopped in the shower for three solid minutes, then had the quickest moisturizing situation I'd encountered in my life, along with a couple sprays of perfume.

Thankfully, I'd gotten braids this past weekend, so I wouldn't have to fiddle too much with my hair.

I would not have time for a full face, but I could do half a face in the car. I got my little pallet and tossed it on the bed next to my clutch then got dressed in record time. I glanced at my watch. I still had ten minutes.

Okay, I guessed I could do my makeup.

I was slapping on the primer when Morgan came running in. "Hey, are you okay?"

"Yep, why?"

"It's just that you barely said a word to Lucy."

Chapter 19

"Yeah, I'm good. We had a weird interaction at the engagement party, but it doesn't matter. You're interviewing her for your paper. I just wish I'd known she was coming to the house."

"Oh." Morgan looked worried. "I'm sorry. Atticus said I could have anyone over that I wanted. I didn't think to ask permission. But obviously, she's been cleared."

I sighed, tapping my sister's face. "We're fine. I was just surprised, that's all. And you can have anyone you want over. I promise. Besides, I'm Mrs. Price now. So any weirdness is kind of over."

"Okay. I just wanted to check." She stepped back and whistled low. "You are stunning. I hate the fact that you barely need any makeup."

"I'll do my eye makeup in the car. I just want to get a basic face on."

I brushed my brows and then shoved the rest of the makeup that I would need into my clutch. I did a little twirl. "What do you think?"

"You are beautiful, sister. You look like you're getting married. I dig that."

"What shoes do you think?"

"Manolos, obviously."

"Not the Louise Vuittons?"

She shook her head. "No. Definitely Manolos."

She jogged into the closet to pull out the exact shoe that

she was looking for. Pink and white with a single jewel at the back of the heel.

The clutch was pink and matched them effortlessly. "Well, I guess you knew exactly which pair."

"Of course I do. My brother-in-law is very lucky to have you. But just in case, make sure you remind him."

I laughed. "Of course."

I grabbed my clutch, and when I walked back to the living room, Lucy turned around and whistled low. "Wow, you are a vision."

"Thank you. It's lovely of you to say so. I'm so sorry I can't stay and chat, but obviously, Morgan knows where everything is. Morgan, Magda is in the building, so if you need something just call her and she'll come up and prepare anything you want."

Lucy laughed. "Oh, trust me, I'm well aware of Magda. And I know where everything is."

I ground my teeth at that. Of course she did. She'd been here before. She was the old me. "Right. Well, have a good night."

I jogged around the dining room, past the kitchen, and back toward the entrance before I realized the damn tickets for the art show we were attending after dinner were in my work bag.

I ran back to the living room. Morgan was walking down the hall by her room, but I didn't see Lucy with her. Where had she gone?

Chapter 19

I stomped down the hall and into our room only to find her coming out of the bathroom. "Oh, what did you forget?" she asked casually.

I frowned at her. "Did you need something?"

"Yeah, I was just using the bathroom."

My bathroom? Every single bedroom in the penthouse had a bathroom, and there was a powder room in the hallway.

"Okaaaay." A familiar scent hit my nose. It smelled like Atticus. Granted, I just used the shower, but it smelled like his cologne.

You're being paranoid.

I grabbed my work bag, grabbed the tickets, and then I scooted her out of our room.

"Oh, I'm sorry. I didn't mean to overstep. I shouldn't have used your bathroom. I should have just waited for Morgan and used the powder room."

"Yeah, that would make me more comfortable. We have some sensitive items in the bedroom, you know."

"Oh God, I didn't even think about it. I'm sorry. I would never..." Her voice trailed off. She would never, what? Snoop? Pry through my things? Touch things that don't belong to her? Lay on the bed that I share with my husband? No, of course she wouldn't.

"Of course." But just to be safe, I closed the door and then deliberately locked it.

She lifted a brow.

GWEN

"I can't be too careful, you know, Lucy. My work laptop is there, so—" I let my voice hang right there.

"Oh right, of course. I'm sorry. I should have waited."

Yeah, as we had established. I didn't feel comfortable leaving her there, but I had to go. As I left, I texted Morgan.

Me: *Please don't leave Lucy unattended. I just found her in my bedroom.*

Sissy Face: *What? Why was she in the bedroom?*

Me: *Bathroom.*

I pushed the button rapidly, trying not to let what I'd just seen affect me. But it was nearly impossible. She had been in my bedroom. A place I was sure she was more than familiar with.

20

GWEN

I was supposed to be having a good time.

Dinner was delicious. The wine and food were amazing. Atticus had taken me to a friend's restaurant. It was a new French spot and very lively, highlighting foods from all over the world where there were French-speaking people. But I had been distracted. At the art gallery, Atticus leaned over and said, "Okay, what's the problem? I thought you wanted a night out, but you seem distracted. Annoyed maybe?"

His brow was furrowed and his gaze was unsure, as if trying to ascertain what he'd done wrong.

I sighed. "Oh shit, I'm sorry. I am distracted, but that is not your fault. That's on me. I'm with you. I promise."

His gaze swept over me. "You look beautiful. I did tell you right? That's all I've been thinking about. How much you can shift your dress and how much of a peek I'll get."

I had to chuckle at that. "Atticus, stop."

"What? You're teasing me with all that skin on display."

"It's barely any cleavage."

"That thing is slit to your navel."

"Yes, but my breasts are completely covered," I protested.

He smiled. "But it's the hint and the tease of it all. You're killing me."

The adoration in his face was enough to draw a genuine smile out of me. "I'm sorry. I'm here with you. I promise."

He traced his thumb over my knuckles. "Come on, Ness, talk to me. What's that phrase you always say to me? Use your words."

I allowed him to pull me into his arms. "I'm sorry. You worked so hard to make tonight fun and nice, and I have been distracted."

"I don't care that you're distracted. I mean I *do* care, but I want to know why. What's going on? When I saw you last at the office, you were really excited about the latest progress that you made and with the lessons that Micah was giving you on the company holdings. I'm not sure how that's at all interesting, but you were happy. What happened between then and now? Is Jack being a pain in the ass?"

Jack now reported to me, which he didn't like so much, and it made him a bit slow to respond.

"I worked a little longer than I thought, and I was late heading back to the penthouse to change. And when I walked in, Lucy was there with Morgan."

Chapter 20

He released me and took a shocked step back. "What?"

"Yeah, Lucy, your ex. The bitchy one from our engagement party. She was there."

He muttered under his breath and immediately pulled out his phone, but I stopped him. "No, it's not like she snuck in there. Morgan's interviewing her. It's for a school project, something about the oldest charity foundations in the city that are still running. I don't know more details than that."

"Fuck. How was she cleared?"

I winced, not wanting to get anyone in trouble. "I think she's on the clearance list from before."

Another curse under his breath. "I'll fix it. I swear to God I will fix it. You shouldn't have to feel like that."

I released a sharp breath. "That's the thing. I'm not sure if she *made* me feel uncomfortable or if I felt that way out of pure jealousy about her being in my house, knowing she's been there before."

"She has been there before, but she never stayed over—"

"No, I'm not saying that. I'm trying to get, you know, used to *us*, and it was a bit disconcerting to walk in and find her in our house. And when I realized I'd forgotten the tickets and went back to get them... I know I sound so silly, but she was in our bathroom, I think."

His furrowed brows turned into a deep frown. "What do you mean she was in our bathroom?"

"I sound crazy. I *know* I sound crazy. Well, crazy is the wrong word. Because I'm allowed to have an emotional reaction to seeing your ex in my house. I just didn't like how it made me feel. I'm sorry. It's made me weird, and I just keep stewing over it. Let's just forget it and have a good time."

He opened his mouth like he was going to argue. But then he closed it. And he nodded. The rest of the evening was spent mostly normally, as I tried desperately to focus. Because God, I did want to focus. It had been a long time since we'd had an actual date night that wasn't work or that wasn't at La Table Ronde with everyone else. Just us, with the intention of being fun and connected.

Atticus had attempted to give me some sense of normalcy, and for the most part, it worked.

As we made our way toward Serendipity, I said, "I think it's closed."

Atticus winked. "You underestimate me."

When we walked up to the door, the restaurant was in fact closed, but the owner unlocked the door to greet us. "Mr. Price, it's good to see you."

"Thank you. You know our order."

He nodded. "Coming right up."

I tugged on his hand. "What did you do?"

"Normally they would be open late tonight. But I bought out the whole place so that you could try as many desserts as you wanted."

"What?"

"Yeah, I was arranging it when you went to the bathroom at the gallery."

Chapter 20

"Atticus, I love you."

"I know. I mean, I have loved you for longer than you've loved me, but we won't quibble."

I laughed. "What are you talking about?"

"It doesn't matter."

It did make me think about what he meant by that though. He had relentlessly pursued me. But that wasn't love; that was lust, right?

It was interesting to be chased. It had never happened before. Lance didn't necessarily count because he was always just there as my friend. In those moments where it looked like it might tip into something else, something always happened to make it stop from going there. But the way Atticus had been single-mindedly focused on me, that was different.

By the time we got home, I was happy and buzzing from the sugar high, and I had put Lucy out of my mind. Until we stepped back in the penthouse.

In the foyer, Atticus took my hands. "You got tense again."

"Sorry. But you know what? Why don't you take me to our bedroom and make me forget all about her," I said suggestively.

"Okay, I think I can make that happen."

I halfway expected to find Lucy in my living room, still sitting there, eating our snacks and watching our TV, but she wasn't there, thank God. We found a note on the corner of the dining room table from Morgan that said she'd gone to bed and please not to wake her by breaking any of the furniture because we were fucking on it.

I so wanted to laugh. "Oh my God."

Atticus read the note over my shoulder. "I think she underestimates us. We don't need to break the furniture for me to fuck you on every surface in here."

"Oh, Mr. Price, you do tempt a girl."

With a teasing laugh, he took me to our room, but he sobered when he discovered the door was locked. "Where was she?" he asked as he let us in.

I pointed at the bathroom.

"Is that why you locked the door?"

"Yes. I didn't want her to steal anything. My laptop was in here, and I don't trust her."

"And that's smart. Your instincts are never off, Gwen. If you think something's up, then something is up, I trust your instincts implicitly."

I hadn't known how much I needed to hear those words until that moment. "Thank you," I said sincerely.

"In case it's a mystery, you are my North Star, Gwen. You are all I think about, all I dream about. When I see my future, it's only you, our children, the work we can do, what we can build. The good we can do for the world. You shouldn't feel off kilter or concerned because you own me body and soul. I already gave you my empire, but my heart and my body have been yours since you glitter-bombed me

Chapter 20

on a balcony. I will tell you this every single day until you *feel* it, not just know it. In the meantime, I want to erase the presence of her being in our bedroom from your mind. And I am going to talk to Morgan about letting us know ahead of time when she's going to have a guest so you won't get surprised again."

"Why are you so good to me?"

"Because you make me feel like a whole man. All those little holes in my soul from before are gone. Because of you."

Tugging me toward the bed, he sat me down on it, and I leaned back on my palms, watching him as he shed his jacket and tossed it somewhere behind him. Then he unbuttoned his shirt and tugged off his tie. But what made my eyebrows raise was him planting the tie across his wrist and then very deftly using his fingers and his teeth to tie himself at the wrist.

"I'm giving you full access to my body, Gwen. It's always been yours, but it seems you need a reminder of that. So I'm all yours. Tie me to the bedpost and do whatever you want with me. You don't need to ever feel unsure of my love. Where you go, I go."

I stared at him. "Wait, you're going to let me tie you up?"

"Well, technically I tied myself up, but I'm going to let you tie me to the bedpost and do anything you want to me."

I searched his eyes for any sign of hesitation. "Anything? You're not going to break free?"

"Well, anything within reason. If I think you're in danger

or the penthouse is on fire or something, that's different. But yeah, do whatever you want."

I stood then, turned him around, and eagerly pushed him back on the bed, eliciting a laughing *oof* from him.

"Atticus Price, you don't know what you just agreed to."

21

ATTICUS

My voice was a low rumble when I said, "I'll be a good boy. Do your worst."

With a wicked smile, Gwen reached for the silk tie that bound my wrist. "Oh, I intend to, Mr. Price."

As she secured the tie around my other wrist and the ornate bedpost, a strange sensation overtook me as a shiver ran through me. A combination of vulnerability and anticipation had my heart hammering in my chest, my breathing coming out unevenly as Gwen hiked up her skirt and shimmied down my body.

She straddled me effortlessly, her skirt hiking up and revealing a teasing hint of lace underneath. I watched her with rapt attention, all pretense of composure lost as she leaned forward to plant a soft kiss on my chest, her eyes never leaving mine.

Fuck. I had talked a big game, but I was already on the brink of madness. All vestiges of control slipping out of my hands like water.

"Are you going to drive me insane tonight?" My voice sounded like a feral growl as I spoke. Which was fitting, because I was losing my shit, and she hadn't even started yet.

Her lips curved into an inscrutable smile. "Maybe," she whispered before she bent down, trailing hot kisses down my stomach until her lips hovered above the sensitive spot just below my navel.

I held my breath, tugging against the restraints, suddenly rethinking my idea. I needed to touch her. I was going to die if I didn't.

And she'll let you go... But she'll demand you beg first.

I squeezed my eyes shut, thinking that maybe if I didn't see what she was doing it might help. It didn't. But there was no way I was giving in. Not so soon.

Her lips barely brushed against me once before she suddenly stopped and looked up at me with a teasing glint in her eyes.

She took hold of the waistband of my pants and slowly unbuttoned them, drawing out each second with torturous precision. The sound of the zipper felt like a gong in the silence of our bedroom.

I wasn't going to make it. Fuck, she was killing me, and she hadn't even started yet.

Biting her lip, she dragged my pants down, having to

Chapter 21

reach inside and adjust my cock as she tugged. When she had them to my knees, her gaze pinned on the length of my throbbing dick. A drop of pre-cum leaked from the tip as if in greeting.

"Gwen..." My voice trailed as my remaining brain cells fried. She took my dick into her delicate palm, and I nearly lost it right there. Her touch was molten hot. Firm yet gentle, stoking the fire that threatened to consume us both.

Slowly, so goddamned slowly, she lowered her head. Her breath was a tease over the tip of my cock, and I couldn't help it. I lifted my hips in a plea.

The heat of it almost undid me as I tugged against the restraints, a primal instinct urging me to bury my hands in her hair and pull her down until my cock hit the back of her throat. But I couldn't, not with the silk binding my wrists firmly to the bedpost.

"What's the matter, Mr. Price? Cat got your tongue?" Her voice was as sweet as honey, laced with a heavy note of amusement.

"Fuck, baby, please. Just—" I lifted my hips in frustration.

"Didn't take you long to beg."

Teasing me, she smiled as she took my cock, licking the pre-cum off with the tip of her tongue. When she moaned, swallowing me down, that was it. "Fuck, okay, you win. I beg. Give me your mouth, baby. Fuck Gwen, give it to me."

Her laughter was a soft vibration against my hard length,

sending jolts of electricity through me. "I thought you'd never ask, Atticus."

With those words, she closed her mouth around me, sucking deep. A strangled moan tumbled from my lips as I fought the urge to buck up into her mouth. Held prisoner by my restraints and the expert work of her tongue, there was nothing to do but surrender completely.

Her movements were slow at first, teasing with every lick and suck. She held me captive with her eyes, watching with a devilish delight as I writhed beneath her. My heart pounded in my ears as she took me in deeper and deeper.

Hot.

Wet.

Consuming.

"God, Gwen... Fuck," I groaned breathlessly, my body tight. I felt like she'd lit me on fire from the inside. The fire low in my gut had started to spread, and I tugged on my restraints to no avail.

She hummed around me, the vibration sending sparks of pleasure coursing through my body. My hands clenched around the silk tie that bound me as I felt the pressure inside of me building up to an unbearable level.

Gwen looked up at me from where she was knelt between my spread legs, her eyes full of unbridled desire. Her lips twisted into a wicked smile before she swallowed down on me again, increasing the pace until it was merciless.

Chapter 21

"You like that?" she purred against my skin. She didn't need an answer, and yet, how could I not give her one?

"Fuck, yes," I growled through gritted teeth. "Don't stop. So good. Fuck." I thrashed in the bed, sweat popping on my brow.

She didn't break eye contact once. Those stormy eyes both a challenge and a promise as she continued to torture me with her mouth. Every stroke sent me spiraling closer and closer to the edge.

"Give it to me," she demanded between licks. Her eagerness sparked something primitive within me. This was not just about pleasure; it was about claiming and being claimed in return.

The heat in my belly coiled tighter, and she seemed to sense it. The rhythm of her movements changed, no longer teasing but purposeful, intent on driving me over the edge. She took me down to the base of my cock and my eyes rolled to the back of my head.

I was helpless against the mounting pleasure, my fingers digging deep into the restraints that held me. My breath came out in ragged pants as I chased the oblivion she so skillfully offered.

Her name echoed in the room as a guttural groan tore from my lips. The world narrowed down to Gwen's mouth and her tongue, determined to make me snap.

I watched in a desperate daze as she took more of me into her mouth, her cheeks hollowing out as she sucked. It was the sexiest fucking thing I had ever seen, her mouth a complete revelation and my undoing.

As I bucked my hips upward, desperate for more, she backed off slightly, just to tease me further before deep-throating me again. I groaned at the back of my throat, the sounds guttural and desperate.

"Is that what you want?" she paused to ask, her voice tender yet taunting. Despite the lust clouding my senses, I could hear the smirk in her voice. She owned me.

"Gwen..." I gasped out, on the verge of incoherence. "Don't—stop."

She continued with a renewed vigor, each movement of her head sending waves of pleasure through my body as she took me deeper into her mouth. Her tongue was working wonders, swirling around me, making me delirious.

And then she released me with a pop. I was so far gone I snarled at her. "Get back here."

She shook her head, and frustrated, I tugged at my restraints. When she sat up, she stripped out of her dress. And when she shimmied out of her panties, I salivated.

Eyes on her breasts, I tried to will one of the blackberry-tipped nipples into my mouth. "Come here, wife."

"You, husband, need to learn some patience." She climbed back onto the bed, shimmying up my body to straddle me. When she turned her back to me, her gorgeous ass on display, fuck my life... I almost came right there.

She continued to tease me, swaying her hips seductively

Chapter 21

as the scent of her arousal filled the room. I could only groan in response, hands flexing uselessly around my restraints.

"Patience," she repeated again, sounding supremely pleased with herself. She lowered herself onto my thighs, the heat of her body searing me. My heart pounded out a savage rhythm against my rib cage, anticipation coiling tight in my gut.

Then slowly, torturously so, she started to lower herself onto me, her back arched and head thrown back in ecstasy. The sight of her taking me was more intoxicating than any drink I'd ever had. I bucked upward instinctively, groaning at the sensation of her enveloping me.

"Holy fuck..." I gasped out as she began to ride me. "Your pussy is so good. So perfect. Fuck, Ness. You ride me so good. This fucking view. You trying to make me crave that pretty ass again?"

She swiveled her hips and Christ almighty, my control snapped.

My vision blurred as she drove me deeper into her. I tasted the metallic tang of blood where I'd bitten my lip in a futile attempt to remain composed. My restraint was reaching its end, and the headboard behind me bore the brunt of my desperation, splintering under the force.

I tugged at the silk tie that bound my wrists. It gave way suddenly and a wave of satisfaction coursed through me as I was finally free. Not wasting a moment, I gripped her waist tightly, helping guide her movements as she continued to take me deeper.

With my hands free, I sat up and palmed her full tits, relishing the way she overflowed my big hands. The feeling of her surrounding me intoxicated me. Each time she came down on me, the movement sent sparks flying behind my eyes and a surge of pleasure rippling through me.

"Fuck Gwen... You're so beautiful," I breathed out, my fingers digging into the soft flesh as I thrust up into her. My other hand found its way to one of those blackberry-tipped nipples. I flicked it gently, drawing a sharp gasp from her lips which melted into a long moan.

I switched my attention to her neglected breast, running my thumb over the hardened nipple, causing her to shiver. The sight was so erotic that it drove me fucking insane.

That was Gwen—my wife—commanding me with just the sway of her hips. How she reveled in it. And why shouldn't she? She held power over me that no one else did.

The way Gwen moved was hypnotic, a sultry dance meant for my eyes alone. She threw her head back in pleasure, her lithe body gleaming in the moonlight that streamed through our bedroom window.

I watched as beads of sweat trickled down her neck and then down her back. Tendrils of her hair escaped her braids, making her look like the goddess she was.

Fuck, I was losing it. I fisted a hand in her hair, the other

Chapter 21

on her shoulder, tugging her head back and bringing her down hard on my cock.

"Mine," I growled into her ear, losing myself deeper into her. "My wife. My. Fucking. Wife."

She replied with a throaty moan that nearly had me undone. "Always."

Our movements became more frantic as we chased our climax, the intensity mounting with each thrust.

"Yours, Atticus. Always." Her voice was thick with desire, the words seeming to lengthen out the vowels in a breathy whisper. I could feel her tightening around me in response, and my grip on her tightened.

"Yes," I groaned, giving her one hard thrust. "Don't forget it, Mrs. Price. Fuck, I love fucking you."

She answered me with a throaty laugh and began to ride me harder, each movement causing delicious friction that had me gasping for breath. My eyes rolled back at the sensation, my hands desperately clutching at her hips as I fought to keep up with her rhythm.

My awareness narrowed down to just Gwen and the way her body moved against mine. Each movement of her hips was an invitation, a provocation that had my breath hitching and my heart pounding.

"Fuck... Gwen..." The words were torn from me, involuntary noises of pleasure as she took me deeper within her.

Suddenly, her rhythm faltered, her body tensing as a cry of pleasure tore its way from her throat. I felt it too—the sudden tightening around me, the tremors coursing through her as she came, pulsing around me. It was the most erotic thing I'd ever seen, my wife surrendering to the pleasure I gave her.

"Atticus!" she cried out, her voice hoarse with pleasure.

The sight of her, the sounds she made, the feel of her clenching around me... It was enough to push me over the edge. With a guttural groan, I followed her into bliss, my body shuddering as waves of satisfaction washed over me.

"Gwen..." My voice was shaky as I buried my face into the crook of her neck, my heart hammering in my chest as I held onto her. "Jesus fucking Christ." I was blind. I was certain of it.

No dumbass, you just can't open your eyes right now, you're so exhausted.

I peeled them open to find my wife looking at me with a mischievous grin on her face and a dark braided curl flopping on her brow. "So much for staying in the handcuffs, Mr. Price."

The low chuckle tumbled out of its own accord. "What can I say? I might have lost control a little."

"Mmm, I like it when you lose control," she murmured, before dropping her head to my shoulder.

One of her aftershocks rippled around my cock and I groaned as my cock stirred. "Fucking hell, woman, you're going to kill me with pleasure."

Her only answer was a moan as I shifted us to our sides. I

Chapter 21

slowly started to pull out of her, but she tightened around me with a whimper.

"No," she moaned, holding onto me tighter. "Stay... just a little longer."

I chuckled. "If I stay, I'll fuck you again. You'll be sore."

Another whimper. "But, I need..." her voice trailed and her hips shifted.

"What do you need, baby?"

"I think I still need..."

I slid my hand down her hip, and between her thighs again. She was so slick from both of us.

"Is this what you need? More?"

"Yes. God. I want more."

"Greedy little wife." I dipped a finger into her sweet cunt, coating my finger with our cum.

Her moan was the only response. I grinned, leaning in to whisper in her ear, "Beg me."

"Atticus," she whimpered, writhing beneath my touch. "I need you. Please."

"You're going to be the death of me," I murmured in her ear before sliding a finger into her, delighted by the slickness that welcomed me. She gasped and squirmed, pressing into my hand.

I took the warm slick wetness, and stroked her clit.

Her body jerked, her breath hitching in a sharp intake. She grabbed my wrist, pressing it harder against her.

"Yes! Please...," she groaned, her body shuddering under

my touch. The air was heavy with lust and our mixed scents of sex.

"Good girl," I whispered into her ear, giving her clit another firm stroke before slipping two fingers inside her. She gasped at the sudden intrusion but didn't pull away. Instead, she pushed herself further onto my hand, moaning loudly as I began to move my fingers in a steady rhythm.

"Oh God...Atticus," she finally managed to pull herself together. Her voice was shaky, filled with desire and need. I watched as she bit her lower lip, her fingers clutching the sheets beneath us.

"That's it, baby," I murmured into her ear, my voice husky.

Her eyes rolled back and she let out a strangled gasp. "Atticus!" She cried out my name as an orgasm ripped through her body. She shook violently under me, clenching my fingers inside her while waves of pleasure washed over her.

I continued to stroke her through her orgasm until finally, she stopped shuddering and collapsed onto the bed, breathless and sated.

Slowly, I pulled my fingers out of her, watching as she shivered from the aftershocks.

I leaned down over her, pressing a soft kiss to her lips. "My greedy little wife. Now, let me get you a towel."

I slipped out of bed, striding naked to the en-suite bath-

Chapter 21

room. I picked up a fluffy, white washcloth from the rack and wet it with warm water.

Back in the bed, I found her curled up on her side, her eyes closed but a satisfied smile lingering on her parted lips. Her hair was messy, tangled with perspiration and the exertion of our lovemaking. A thin sheet barely covered her, the outline of her naked form visible beneath it. Beautiful.

After cleaning her up quickly and tossing the towel in the basket, I climbed back into bed with her, pulling her to me.

"I love you, Atticus."

"I know. And I love you, Mrs. Price."

22

ATTICUS

La Table Ronde was crowded as usual, but our normal spot had been reserved.

In front of me, Gwen sashayed through the restaurant, and my gaze slid down to focus on her ass. Goddamn, it was a thing of beauty.

"I can feel you watching me, Mr. Price," she said cheekily over one shoulder.

"Yeah, well, if you don't like it, stop sashaying for me, Mrs. Price."

We were led into one of the back rooms for a private dinner and found the guys were already there.

Morgan was in the corner sulking because it seemed Lance wouldn't let her have a drink. She nodded as we walked in and immediately began complaining to her sister. "Gwen, your idiot best friend won't let me have a drink."

Chapter 22

Gwen didn't miss a beat. "Morgan, sweetheart, you're not twenty-one yet."

There was a chorus of "oooohs" and "aaaahs" when the food was brought in, and everyone grabbed the small plates and settled in as we started to look over the files.

Pierce sat back and wiped his mouth as he grabbed the remote, using a large monitor mounted on the wall to show us where we were.

"Looks like the Mangles kid came through. Because thanks to Gwen's algorithm, I got a good look from the camera right here at the bank"—he indicated a spot on-screen—"and we have a visual of the shooter."

We all leaned in.

Lance piped up. "I cleaned it up as much as I could."

Gwen took a large sip of her drink. "It's a simple search then. I can run facial recognition and we should find this asshole in no time. Then I can get my life back."

I didn't know what it was, but I couldn't keep my eyes off my wife. There was something in her smile, the way she interacted with each of my friends, the ease of being with her. This was what family felt like.

I glanced over in the corner, wondering what Morgan and Lance were fighting about this time. Was I supposed to do something about that now? She was my sister. She had said that she was happy she now had a big brother, but did that include interference?

I had no idea how to navigate that. Micah had been easy.

Honestly, most of the time I thought the kid was smarter than I was, but he had wanted a big brother, so he tagged along everywhere behind me. It was easy to look out for him in most instances.

Except with your father.

I glanced over at Gwen to see if she was clocking what was happening, but she was engaged in an animated conversation with Gavin about his daughter. I'd have to figure out the Morgan situation later.

Reaching out absently, I stroked my wife's shoulder, and the shift in her weight toward me made me smile.

When I raised my gaze, Micah was lifting a brow at me. I just shrugged at him and grinned. Then he gave me a knowing nod and turned his attention back to whatever the hell Rowan had been saying.

Gwen's laptop finally beeped and she stood. "We've got a match."

My gut twisted as I considered it. The sooner we could get this fucker off the street, the better. So why was I suddenly anxious?

"A Peter Reeser?" Gwen said with a question in her voice.

She glanced up at me as if I knew him. But I immediately shook my head and said, "It doesn't ring a bell." I turned my attention to my brother, who also shook his head. It was my secondary gaze to Pierce that had my stomach twisting.

Chapter 22

"I know the name," he said, his voice low. "He's an assassin."

"An assassin?" I asked, not really surprised, given how efficient he'd been.

Pierce's gray eyes were clear but grave. "Yeah, one I know by name."

My gut knotted. Pierce had seen a lot of shit. Shit I didn't even know about. Things he couldn't talk about. I knew that during those years that he'd gone dark from my life he'd been through some stuff. But now he knew assassins?

"That means he was hired," I said, stating the obvious. "Which means Dad is still in play."

Micah nodded. "I'll go talk to him."

I shook my head. "You are the last person who needs to talk to Dad."

The firm line of Micah's lips told me just what he thought of that, but I didn't give a fuck. I wasn't letting him talk to the old man. I'd talk to him.

You mean kill him?

Gavin, being Gavin, volunteered. "Look, how about *I* go interview the old man? I'll even notify his lawyer that we need to speak to him, and we can figure out how he knows Reeser."

Pierce cleared his throat then rubbed the back of his neck. "You don't need to do that. Now that I'm seeing a photo of Reeser, I realize I've seen him before."

I frowned at him. "What the fuck do you mean you've seen him before? From your old life or recently?"

He dragged in a deep breath. "I know the name from before. But the face is recently familiar."

I shifted in my seat. Automatically, Gwen leaned toward me, as did my brother.

Was I that volatile?

Well, it looks like you might beat your best friend's ass, so it's entirely possible that you are that volatile.

Pierce was scrolling through his phone, and he held a photo out to Gwen. "Is that him?"

Gwen looked back and forth between the image on the screen and the image on his phone. "Yeah, that is him. Where was that taken?"

Another deep breath from Pierce. "It's from you're engagement party. He was there that night."

I glared at him. "He was there? At my engagement party to Gwen?"

"Yes," he said hesitantly.

"Do you mean to tell me that we had an assassin under our noses during the engagement party? How did that happen? How is Gwen even still alive?"

"I don't know," Pierce said in frustration. "We vetted everyone who walked through those doors. Something is very, *very* wrong."

Gwen reached out and took my hand in hers. I resisted the urge to pull away, to shield her in some way from my

Chapter 22

fury. But instead of that dark coldness that usually slid into place, she chased it off with her warmth.

It was a happy warmth, keeping me calm enough to use my words instead of my fists. "Would you fucking find out?"

Gwen spoke up. "I can help."

Pierce shook his head. "No. With all due respect, I fucked up, and I'll fix it."

Lance glanced from me, to Pierce, then to Gwen, and back to Pierce again. "I'll help. I know Gwen's software well. I can double check all the facial recognition data from that night. And I'm a decent hacker. It'll go faster."

Pierce nodded and lifted his gaze back to mine. "I'm sorry, Atticus. I'll fix it. I promise."

I didn't have any words for him. He needed to fucking fix it. This was Pierce. I needed to be able to count on him.

Mistakes like this don't happen with Pierce. He's too good at his job. So if he's making mistakes, you have to ask yourself why.

And I would eventually take it a step further. Not just why, but what the hell else had he missed?

23

ATTICUS

"Atticus Price, are you sulking?"

I frowned at my wife, looking absolutely gorgeous in her gray pantsuit, the top of which cut off just an inch above where the pants sat, showing a strip of skin that made me want to run my hands under her jacket and cup her breasts...

I blinked rapidly. "What did you say?"

She narrowed her gaze at me, and I gave her a sheepish grin. "Were you listening to me, Atticus, or were you too busy plotting?"

"Yeah, of course I was. You said something, something, about something."

"Atticus, that's not funny."

"Yes, love, I was listening to you. And I'm not plotting."

"Okay then, tell me that you won't try to murder your

Chapter 23

father. And that it's not going to cause you emotional distress that I'm talking to him."

I clenched my jaw tight and tried to look the one person on earth next to my brother who knew me the best straight in the eye. "I'm not going to murder him."

The problem was the word *murder* came out sort of gleefully.

Morgan snorted from the corner of the living room where she perched prettily on the hanging chair Gwen had added a couple of weeks ago.

"Why did it sound like you were so happy about the idea of murder?" Gwen asked.

"I'm not."

Micah, Lakewood, and Gwen audibly scoffed, and Morgan just laughed to herself.

Pierce didn't laugh though, because he was still busy kicking himself over everything that had happened.

"Fine," I turned to my brother. "You're going with her, right?"

Micah nodded. "There's no way I would make anyone handle that alone."

Gwen rolled her eyes. "I can handle him."

I threw my hands up. "Unless he's trying to murder you. The man is a master manipulator. He's been at this for years. So if you're not going to let me murder him, then at least take someone with you when you talk to him."

She rolled her eyes. "All right, that's fair. Who's going with you to talk to Bronson?"

We'd opted to divide and conquer the suspects. The most likely suspects for hiring an assassin to take care of Gwen were my father and Bronson Jacobson. Lucy, while a bothersome problem, was seen as little threat. Her family was off the list. Her father was an asshole, but he had no reason to want Gwen dead. Nevertheless, we'd circle back and take another look at them if nothing panned out with Jacobson or my father. "Fine, who do you deem as my escort?"

Morgan raised a hand. Gwen, Lance, and I all shook our heads. "No, you stay here," I said emphatically.

Morgan rolled her eyes. "God, you guys never let me have any fun."

I couldn't help but chuckle at that, and she stuck her tongue out at me. I had grown men who shook in their boots every single time they had to address me, but this kid was sticking her tongue out at me. I lifted a brow and she just flashed a grin at me, completely unperturbed.

I knew I liked the kid.

" Wait," Gwen said thoughtfully. "Can you be counted on not to murder Bronson?"

I considered it for a moment and started to smile. I saw Morgan point at me. "Look, he's thinking the murder thing again."

I waved a hand in dismissal. "I've already dealt with

Chapter 23

Bronson once, and I didn't murder him then. See? I have shown restraint in the past."

She rolled her eyes. "Lance, go with him."

Lakewood frowned. "Why am I always getting paired with him?"

He said it like a whiny, recalcitrant teenager, and I rolled my eyes. "Gear up, Lakewood. You're my trusted knight."

Gwen laughed at that. "Well, isn't this fun? We are a team again, just like in the Winston Isles."

Gavin chuckled. "Um, I have been given no job."

Rowan shoved macaroons in his mouth that Gavin had made as he returned from the kitchen. "I don't have a job either."

I smiled at both of them and then back at Morgan.

Morgan whined. "Oh my God, I do not need an escort."

"Yes, you do, kid. You have to go to a family dinner with the Beckers."

Gwen frowned. "Ugh, I'd forgotten about that." She made a sweet face at her sister. "I'm sorry, Morgs. You think you can handle him on your own?"

Morgan shrugged. "I should be fine. Besides, I'll have eye candy with me."

That made Gavin blush, and Rowan grinned back at her until I growled at him. Then his grin fell.

Morgan chose that moment to scowl at me. "You're ruining all my fun."

I turned back to Rowan. "No hands."

Rowan blinked in surprise. He was young, and unlike most of the men Pierce hired, he was straight out of school. So he was close enough to Morgan's age for me to be worrying. She was my sister. I was supposed to worry about her, wasn't I?

She just rolled her eyes. "Right, and I will stay put."

When the team broke apart, Lakewood was right on my heels. "So, partner, how are we going to do this? Bad cop, good cop? I was really thinking, bad cop, bad cop personally, because you already got a bite out of him. At the time he was being such an asshole to her, Gwen wouldn't let me do anything. So I'm hoping for retribution this time."

I was liking Lakewood a lot better now. "Well, let's hope we actually get information from him. And then, if you take off his head, I won't care. Hell, I'll provide you an alibi."

"With all due respect, Price, you should *be* the alibi."

As it turned out, Jacobson wasn't hard to find. We didn't call ahead, but he wasn't in the office or at home. And then Lakewood had an idea. He'd pulled up the latest hookup app and then made a quick fake profile using photos he grabbed from the internet. With a few well-placed keywords, I got favorite places and favorite restaurants to match Bronson Jacobson's. Places that he had either taken Gwen to or frequented. He suddenly showed up in a pool of men. Lakewood set himself as available. And suddenly, there was a match and a location for a meet-up all set up. At a hotel, obviously.

Chapter 23

"Do people really use this thing?" I asked, inquiring about the dating app.

He shrugged. "Seems like a sad way to find a mate, but for people just looking to hookup, it's the new thing."

I frowned. "God, it's so easy to meet women. Why would anyone do this?"

"Well, not everyone is Atticus Price," Lakewood said. "Some guys have to work harder. Women threw themselves at you all the time, hoping for a chance to be Mrs. Atticus Price. You had your pick of women who would do anything you wanted just to prove to you that they were wife material."

"That's ridiculous."

"Yes, it is. I mean, look, I'm not complaining. I know I get the benefits of the Lakewood name."

"Yeah, about that, did you figure out what you're going to do about your grandfather's will?"

He shook his head. "I'm not going to think about that right now. I'm ignoring it until I don't have to."

I shrugged. "Fair."

"Let's go on our date."

It turned out, Bronson was temporarily staying at the Waldorf. As I already had some suites booked there for the incoming executives, I breezed by check-in security with no issues. We reached Jacobson's room and knocked on the door. I shook my head when he opened it so easily.

"Christ, Jacobson, you didn't even check the peephole?

Just waiting for some random hookup girl to walk in. That, my friend, apparently is how you get—" I turned to Lakewood. "What did Morgan say?"

"Rowed. That's what the kids are saying."

I grinned at Jacobson. "Yeah, that's how you get rowed."

Jacobson tried to shut the door in our faces, but between myself and Lakewood, he couldn't keep us out.

"What the fuck do you two want?"

"Just to have a conversation."

He glared at me. "I've already told you I don't want to see you."

I waived my hand. "Oh, we're going to have a perfectly lovely conversation. Besides, if anything happens to you, everyone will see that you used the hookup app. You really can't be too careful these days."

"What do you want, Price? You said to stay away from Gwen, and I have."

Lakewood made himself comfortable on the edge of the bed. That made Jacobson distinctly uncomfortable. "What the fuck do you want?"

"Peter Reeser. What do you know about him?" I asked.

"Who?"

"Peter Reeser," Lakewood said with an air of 'I'm really not here to fuck with you.' I might not like him, but when it came to Gwen, he did not play around.

"I have done what you asked, haven't I? I heard you loud

Chapter 23

and clear, Price. Don't fuck with your wife. Understood. Message received."

"You say that." I paced in front of him slowly, as if I had all the time in the world. But I needed him to fucking start talking. "Except, you didn't get the message the first time, and you tried to talk to her."

"I haven't approached her. Ask her, she'll fucking tell you."

"That's the thing, why should I have to bother Gwen with such frivolity? Because if you hired someone to try and kill her…"

Jacobson put his hands up and started backing up. "Fuck, no I didn't. I'm not insane."

"Sure, you are. You tried talking to her after I told you not to." I prowled toward him, and he continued to back up. And Lakewood added to the effect by just lazing sadistically on the bed.

"I was pissed, yeah. You cost me millions. But try to kill her? You're already fucking unhinged, man. I'm not trying to invite more trouble."

"Why should I believe you?"

"I don't know this guy, Reeser."

I leaned in real close. "You're sure? Because hiring an assassin is easy. It's exactly the kind of bitch move that you would make."

Jacobson frowned. "No. It wasn't me. Her father, maybe. He's desperate enough to do something like this. Not me."

I turned to Lakewood. "Funny how when he's desperate, he will find anyone else to take the fall."

"I mean, it doesn't make a ton of sense," Lance mused, "but at least he gave us something to look at."

"Do you believe him?" I asked.

"You've already shown him that you can ruin him. Besides, I think you and your boys already have him pissing himself. He's not dumb enough to make that mistake."

Bronson nodded his head. "Yeah, what Lakewood said. I learned my lesson. I swear I don't know him."

I didn't want to believe him, but I did. He looked scared and like he had no idea what the fuck I was talking about. He wasn't connected to Reeser. And as much as I wanted to kill him, Gwen had been pretty clear on the no-murdering thing.

"Hey, Lakewood, when Gwen said no-murder, do you think she meant you, too?"

Lakewood chuckled low then. "Better not risk it. She's still mad at me for this one time in college when she asked me not to interfere with something and I did. She's still holding a grudge on that one. I would like for her to talk to me sometime in this century." He turned to Jacobson. "So lucky for you, Bronson. You get to live."

In the elevator, I said, "Well, it's a pity that didn't pan out, Lakewood. But hopefully, Gwen and Micah have had more luck with my father."

Chapter 23

His eyes met mine, and we both knew what I meant. If they came up snake eyes on the old man as well, we weren't any closer. And there was an assassin in our midst.

24

GWEN

"Oh look, the prodigal son returns," Lucian Price said sarcastically.

Micah didn't even flinch as he stoically stood next to me. He said nothing.

"Mr. Price, we just have a few questions for you," I began.

His gaze darted back to me. "I don't speak to the help, girl."

I grinned. "Of course, you don't. Good thing I'm your daughter now, *Dad*."

"All because of a deal Atticus made. You're the bride he bought and paid for. And now you're stuck with him."

"Well, consider me the help if you want, but I own majority shares of Pendragon, Dad. So call me what you like, but I'm still richer than you."

Chapter 24

That got a smile from Micah. A quick glance at him told me his lips were twitching. When we finally sat, we could see Lucian's hands cuffed to the table. Micah sat forward and said, "How this goes is we ask the questions, and you answer. No bargaining, and you're not to insult Gwen any more than you already have. We're not here for chitchat. You've already made your bed, and you're going to lie in it."

"You think your charges will stick?"

Micah glowered at him, and I placed a hand over his, giving it a gentle squeeze. "We're not here for a fight. We're here to get questions answered and go," I reminded him.

"Boy, tell the bitch to stop talking to me."

Well, we were off to a great start. "Oh, you will talk to me, whether it's now or later. You see, I'm merely the thing standing between you and your other son doing something drastic. He wanted to pull every string he could to get you locked up in the biggest super max he could find. Atticus will do anything to protect the people he loves. And you are not one of them. After what you did to his mother, he doesn't care what he has to do, because to him there are no rules. Not to mention, the government has questions about tax evasion, fraud, you know how it goes. It would be a shame if they found every single property you had. Not that you're ever going to leave here. But if you did eventually manage to make some kind of appeal and get things overturned, you would have nothing. And I would have everything that you own. I mean, we don't want to go that far. We just want you to pay for what you did to Brian Riley and Atticus's mother. So answer our questions, and we keep Atticus from doing a whole revenge tour."

"You think you can control that boy? He's defective. Just like his brother here."

Again, his insults didn't even faze Micah.

"That's interesting that you would say that, Mr. Price. They're *your* flesh and blood, but it was both of their mothers who made them strong men who managed to escape your evil influence. So there's that."

He rattled his handcuffs in frustration. "I'm bored. Let's get this over with."

"At last, cooperation. Look, it's no mystery that you will do anything to get back at your sons. You clearly have issues. But my question is, what's your problem with me? Up until Atticus gave me control of the company, you didn't have any beef with me. I've done nothing to you."

His brow furrowed. "I don't understand your line of questioning."

I studied him, unable to tell if he was lying.

Micah sat forward. "Enough bullshit. With what you did to Jessica, you're looking at fifteen years at least, but you'll eventually have a chance at getting out and enjoying whatever is left of your miserable little existence. But if you also hired an assassin to kill her, you're never going to see the light of day. And bad things happen to prison inmates all the time," he said threateningly.

Chapter 24

The old man's eyes went wide. "I never fucking hired an assassin to kill Jessica. I didn't want her dead. If she died, all of her shares went straight to Atticus, and that's not what I needed. I needed control of my company."

Micah rolled his eyes. "You mean grandfather's company. Technically, Atticus's, because you were just a seat warmer until Atticus came of age."

"I had no reason to fucking kill his mother."

Micah sighed. "We're not talking about Jessica, anyway. We're talking about Gwen. Did you hire an assassin to kill her?"

Lucian's gaze flickered from his son, to me, and back again. "Someone's trying to kill you? Oh God, this is too brilliant. If you die, my son becomes very, very upset. Tortured even. God, I love that idea. Ahh, this is a fucking delight. Best news I've had all day."

Micah sat back. "He doesn't know anything."

Lucian laughed. "Oh, you think you know me so well. You've come and given me this gift. Maybe I *should* have hired someone to kill this bitch. It would have saved me a lot of headaches, that's for fucking sure."

For some reason, out of everything he'd said, this was the thing that shook Micah's cool. "You are such a hateful fuck."

"And you are a useless, spineless, son of a whore. All my attempts to shape you and mold you did nothing. You still turned out useless. You didn't understand the importance of power. You chose your brother over me. And now what are you, his lackey?"

Micah pushed to his feet. "We're done here."

I nodded. Seeing the effect that this crazy man had on Micah lit a spark of rage inside me. "You know, I've been trying to figure it out, understand why you are the way that you are, and I finally see it. Clear as day. You are jealous of Atticus, of Micah, of the ease of the relationship that they have. The fact that they thrived without you has only made you more envious. The fact that they have more than survived... You can't take it, can you? And now you're sitting in here, and they're out there, running the company that was theirs, given to them by someone better than you. The company you tried to swipe from under their noses. You failed on all accounts, so all you have in here, old man, are your regrets, your envy, and your hatred. And even those are a gift from your sons, because you are still alive."

I turned to Micah. "Maybe we should have just let Atticus do whatever he wanted with him. It would put an end to all of this misery."

As we were about to leave, I turned a level gaze on the man that had hurt the men I cared very much about. "You know, I have a wish for you. That someone shows you the same kind of malice and toxic energy that you reserved for the world. I hope you find that person in here with nothing but hatred and loathing in their heart for you. Matter of fact, I feel like whispering to a guard about some of the women

Chapter 24

who've filed claims against you and how they were perhaps underage. That should take care of it. I hear they don't like pedophiles in prison."

His brows furrowed. "You lying bitch."

I gave him a sweet smile. "Nope. Who said anything about lying? One of the girls who was an intern at Pendragon is barely eighteen, and when I had a look through the records, since I knew we were coming here and would need some leverage, I discovered she was underage when she filed her complaint. And I will make sure every single person in here knows about it. Have a nice rest of your life, Lucian."

25

GWEN

"I really wish you'd let me do it, Atticus."

"For what purpose? He didn't have the information we needed anyway, so there's no point for you to have to live with that."

Atticus had me on the couch in his office, and he'd forced me to take off my shoes so he could rub my feet. There were worse things that could happen.

"Micah said that he was definitely an asshole, but you held your own. I believe that Dad was telling the truth about not hiring anyone to kill you. Obviously, we're going to verify that because it *is* my father."

"And we should verify. But I believed him, too. He didn't know. His game is all surrounding you and your mother and Micah. I can't imagine the horror he put you through."

"You don't have to."

Chapter 25

"I know but my heart still breaks for little Atticus and Micah."

"We're strong now. He can't hurt us anymore. We can protect ourselves, Gwen. He can't touch us. And I'm not going to let anything touch you either. You need to trust me."

"I know. And I do. It just feels like this is going to go on forever, you know?"

"I know. But for the time being, we'll try and focus on us. We got married in a bit of a hurry, if you remember."

I grinned at him as he used his thumb and slid it over the middle of my foot, smoothing it down my arch working out the perma-knot there from the heels I wore constantly. "Oh my God," I moaned.

"Woman, if you don't stop making that sound, you're going to give me ideas. And you said that I'm not allowed to shag you at the office anymore."

"I don't think it sets the best precedent if the CEO and the largest shareholder can't keep their hands off each other."

He brought my foot up close, kissing the arch, and I met his gaze. "So what does this mean? We're no closer to figuring out who wants me dead. All I want to do is focus on us and what we're doing. I don't want to be looking over our shoulders every second of every day. Maybe it's better if I give you back the shares."

He shook his head. "You can't actually give them back. You can request that Micah vote them for you, but you can't give them up. And you and I both know that's not why someone was trying to kill you. Someone tried to do that long before you were the most powerful woman in the tech industry. We just have to figure out who."

His assistant knocked on the door, and Atticus called out, "Come."

Andrew gave me a smile and averted his gaze when he saw my bare feet on Atticus's lap. "Atticus, three minutes until your next call. You're supposed to meet now, but since Gwen is here, do you want me to push it off for twenty minutes?"

Atticus shook his head. "No, I'll take the call if my wife doesn't mind waiting for me."

Honestly, I knew I shouldn't get that warm fuzzy feeling every time he said 'my wife,' but I couldn't help it. "I have things to do. I can't just sit here."

Andrew's gaze volleyed between the two of us, and finally, he just listened to his boss.

Atticus stood, offered me his hand, and then helped me up to my feet. When I reached for my shoes, he shook his head. "No, no. You just come sit with me."

"Oh no, you don't."

"It'll only take a minute. Ten minutes, tops."

"Argh, okay fine. But I have to leave eventually. I have things to do. I need to make sure Jack isn't fucking with my team."

"How is that going?"

Chapter 25

"When I said I needed a redundancy, *he* was not what I meant. I wanted someone competent."

"Then put Macy in charge."

I lifted a brow. "Macy is good. She's extremely smart. She knows the software almost as well as I do. Only caveat is she has no leadership experience."

He shrugged. "Then give her some."

He lifted me up easily, placing me on the edge of his desk. "You sit here." When he took his call, I remembered the last time we were seated like this, him on his call, me showing him what he was missing. I had ten minutes before I had to go down and meet with Jack. Atticus narrowed his gaze at me as he used a pen to flick up the edge of my skirt.

Oh, he wanted another show, did he? Maybe he wasn't going to get a show. Maybe this time, he was going to get the whole she-bang.

Slowly, I lowered to my feet, letting my toes sink into the plush carpeting by his desk. When I lowered to my knees, his eyes went wide, and then his gaze slid to the door.

We forgotten to lock the door again, and since we'd almost gotten caught last time, I reached over and hit the button under his desk, locking us in together.

"Uh-huh. I really want to see those projections."

The timbre of his murmured response on the phone made my clit pulse. It was terse and somewhat foreboding, and it vaguely reminded me of the tone he used when he called me

Ness, when it was dark and just us alone. When I turned around and knelt before him, his teeth grazed his bottom lip, and his gaze never left mine. He knew what this was. He knew what I was planning on doing, and he was all for it.

I unzipped his pants and leaned forward, licking the glistening seam of the tip of his cock, the salty taste of it exploding on my tongue. His hand white-knuckled the arm of his chair as he involuntarily lifted his hips.

Try as he might though, he was unable to conceal his shiver.

He reached over to his phone, hit the speaker button then mute as he put the phone back in its cradle.

"You fucking naughty minx. Is this what you want? My cock?"

I licked delicately again, and his head fell back, his hand going into my hair and fisting tight... almost too tight.

I thought he might try to pull me away, but instead he held me still as he lifted his hips, bringing the tip of his nine-inch cock just inside my pouty mouth.

On the phone, Charles, or whoever, droned on about how beneficial the investment would be financially as I sucked on just the tip of my husband's cock.

"Oh... fuck yes, like that..." Atticus moaned, his eyes clamped shut as he took another deep breath.

Slowly, I took more of him in and used my hand to massage his heavy sac, idly playing with him as I slid my middle finger up and down his cock.

Chapter 25

He unmuted the phone. "We can discuss percentages later..." Then he hit the mute button again as his other hand tightened in my hair. "Gwen..." A warning—no, a plea—laced through his voice as I grinned around his thick girth.

I slid my tongue just underneath the head of his cock, before sucking hard, swirling it around in tight motions as he let out a strangled moan that sounded suspiciously like a curse.

Atticus began to squirm in his seat as I continued to tease him, paying extra attention to the sensitive spot just below the head. His hand continued its vice-like hold on my hair, his body twitching and quaking under my ministrations.

"Mmm, Gwen..." he managed to gasp out, his voice raspy and filled with lust as he fought to keep his eyes open. "My Ness is such a dirty girl. You like having me under your control?"

With a smirk, I released him from my mouth for a moment, staring up into his eyes mischievously. "Oh, I do," I whispered, adding pressure to the hand that was teasing his balls, causing him to let out a muffled groan.

I carefully slid a finger from where it had been teasing him downward, gently applying pressure to his perineum before searching for the entrance to his prostate. A choked moan ripped from his throat as my finger slipped inside of him, and his grip on my hair tightened even more.

With a choked moan and shudder, his mouth fell open, his hard cock swelling on my tongue. "Fuck, fuck, fuck, fuck.

Ness," he ground out through clenched teeth. Then he unmuted the phone, sweat popping on his brow. "W-we can keep discussing the details through email," Atticus hastily said as he struggled desperately to regain control of himself then hung up.

I pulled my mouth off his dick as I tentatively pressed on his prostate.

His body jolted as a thunderous moan echoed in the room. "Shit... Gwen," he half-gasped, half-groaned, his free hand hitting the desk with a thud. My one-handed ministrations were driving him to an edge he'd never experienced before, and I reveled in it.

"Like that?" I murmured against his now moist skin, my tongue flicking out to taste the salty trails of pre-cum that were oozing from his tip.

"Yes. Yes... Fuck... More," he demanded, bucking his hips up and pressing himself deeper into my mouth. His cock twitched as I hit a particularly sensitive spot on his prostate, making me grin around his throbbing length.

In response, I abandoned my slow rhythm and began to bob my head faster along his shaft, my tongue swirling over every vein and ridge. Every so often, I would pull back to suckle on just the tip before swallowing him whole again.

The noises coming from Atticus were raw and primal, filling the room with an intoxicating melody of pleasure. His hand pressed on my head, urging me to take more of him into

Chapter 25

my mouth as he openly groaned at the sensations coursing through him.

In spite of his impending climax, Atticus tried to regain control, his eyes fluttering open to look at me. He watched as I slid my mouth off him slowly, leaving a trail of saliva hanging between us before I swallowed him whole again. Then his back arched, body shaking as his orgasm threatened.

My finger pressed onto his prostate again, and he let out a harsh groan that echoed through the room. His hips snapped up, instinctively seeking more contact as he fought against the pleasure coursing through him.

I loved every moment of this decadent dance between us. The scent of him, his taste, the feel of his twitching cock on my tongue and inside my mouth. I could feel him getting closer to the edge, pulse throbbing under my touch.

"Shit, Gwen." He growled my name again as I increased my speed, bobbing up and down on him roughly now.

His hand was white-knuckled as it held onto the edge of the desk while his other continued its harsh hold on my hair, a silent plea for me not to stop. I felt him quiver under my touch, a sure sign he was on the precipice of sweet release.

"Fuck, Ness," he gasped, his whole body drawn taut and trembling. The veins on his neck popped out and his face flushed deep red as he tried to maintain a semblance of control. His eyes, wide and glossy, were locked onto mine as if I held his very life in my hands.

I maintained eye contact, loving the way his pupils dilated when I pressed down on his prostate. His response was instantaneous and powerful, a loud groan that ricocheted off the walls of the office as my name slipped from his lips like a prayer.

Watching him coming undone was enough to satiate me, but I didn't want to let up just yet. I wanted him begging for release, so I continued with the relentless rhythm of my ministrations.

His body bucked uncontrollably under me, desperate for relief that seemed both within reach and miles away at the same time. His hips were thrusting in sync with every bob of my head now, trying to dictate the pace.

With one final push against his prostate and eager suction from me, Atticus finally let go. He groaned out my name again, louder this time as he rocked up into my mouth desperately.

His grip on my hair tightened as waves of pleasure crashed over him, washing away any coherent thought or control from his mind. His body shuddered beneath me, every twitch and spasm magnified by the tight confines of our intimate embrace.

The spasms racked his body, and I reveled in them, sucking him deeper into my mouth, swallowing down every shot of his release that spilled from him. He seemed lost in pleasure, his deep groans filling the room as he came apart under my touch.

Chapter 25

His face was a beautiful sight, a perfect mix of delicious agony and immense pleasure. His eyebrows were furrowed tightly as he fought to keep his eyes open, not wanting to miss any second of this moment. His mouth hung open in a silent scream, and his breath came out in ragged pants that further heightened the intoxicating atmosphere in the room.

With an earth-shattering moan that echoed around the office, Atticus finally collapsed back into his chair, his hand still gripping my hair as if it were the only thing grounding him. The frenzied pace we'd held moments ago slowed to a relaxed rhythm as he took a moment to come down from his high.

The intimate silence that blanketed us was filled with our staggered breaths and the occasional soft sigh escaping from Atticus's lips. Pulling away slowly, I watched him carefully.

The power shifted back to Atticus after a few moments of panting recovery. He roughly yanked me up his body then sloppily kissed me, unabashed, unconcerned about tasting himself on my lips.

When he pulled back, his eyes were heavy-lidded. "I'm going to tan your ass for that. You could have hurt yourself."

I smirked at him as he gave me another hard kiss. "I'm already more than tan. However will you tell?"

His brows lifted in surprise. "My wife is a brat now? Okay, good to know. I'm going to spank you until you're dripping for me. Then I'm going to spread those beautiful cheeks and fill your ass like you seem to be begging me to."

A shiver of anticipatory pleasure ran down my spine at his words, a delicious promise that sent a fresh wave of desire coursing through me. "Is that so?" I managed to say, trying to sound nonchalant even though my heart was pounding in my chest.

His eyes narrowed as he studied me, clearly not fooled by my blasé tone. "You think I won't do it?" His voice was low and husky, a tone that always made my skin tingle.

"You have another a call, and I have to go. I love you."

His eyes widened at my words, disbelief replacing the roguish spark that had been dancing in his gaze just moments ago. "Gwen..."

26

GWEN

A*TTICUS REACHED* for me and I deftly avoided his grasp. "I have to go."

His phone rang, and his eyes narrowed into slits as he stared at me, trying to pull me into his lap. "I love you." I whispered.

And that was the way I left him. Pants undone, dick out, still hard, looking like he wanted to tear every piece of clothing off my body. Was I horny? Hell, yeah. Was it worth it watching him come completely undone? Absolutely. God, I loved him. Even though things were currently terrifying and scary.

He was making it a point to make me feel loved, make me feel safe. Every action, from making sure to slide smoothies in front of me on the days I left too early to grab food, to making little gummy bear treats appear out of nowhere when things were stressful with my team or when I was poring over files of Pendragon and doing Micah's homework.

He was taking care of me. He was showing me how much he loved me every day, and it was beautiful and fun. And we kept discussing the rule that we weren't going to shag in the office anymore, but honestly, that one was hard to stop.

Technically, I hadn't broken the rule. I had just sucked him off. That was different.

I grinned to myself as I marched out of his office and waived at Andrew. He gave me a broad smile that either said he had no idea what we'd been doing in there and he was just being very friendly, or he knew exactly what we'd been doing in there and he approved of me softening his boss's mood.

"Mrs. Price, erm Gwen, if Mr. Price comes looking for you, where should I tell him you've gone?"

I shook my head at him. "He knows I have a meeting with Jack. I'll just be in my team's bullpen when he's ready to go home."

He gave me a nod. "Okay, I'll tell him."

I gave him a little wave with my fingers and headed down the stairs. Jack shouldn't be left unattended too long. He couldn't ruin much, except my team's morale. I think Atticus was right. While Jack was well intentioned, he was

Chapter 26

not the best guy to manage the team. They didn't want to follow him and he didn't know the software.

He was playing catch-up, and he was used to the kind of positions where he just came in and led teams without having to get into the nitty-gritty of the programming. My team was used to a hands-on leader. He was always going to be a bad fit.

I'd decided I'd walk him through today and then talk to Macy about taking on some leadership responsibilities. I hated the sound my heeled boots made on the stairs as I went down the many flights, but there was no way I was going on the stairs barefoot.

As I approached the fourteenth floor, someone else was opening the door of the stairwell. I just automatically shifted to one side and kept going.

I was already late, and I didn't have time for chitchat. I needed to wash my hands and get a little centered if I was going to deal with Jack for the next hour before we left.

Whoever had opened the door seemed to be heading up instead of down, and I kept moving. When I reached my floor, someone grabbed me from behind. And before I could let out a scream, they had a hand over my mouth and had shoved something dark over my head to obscure my vision, but they didn't get it all the way on before I saw where they were taking me.

I was being dragged into the utility closet right next to

my floor. I was three feet from safety. Three feet from freedom.

I had a guard. Rowan would come and find me. Today was Rowan's day, right? Yes. I'd texted him as soon as I left Atticus's office. It wasn't entirely feasible to have the guys on me at all moments of every day. So they were stationed on our floors. Every single employee of Pendragon had been vetted with an in-depth background check, but my guards were still stationed all over the building just in case.

Like a fool, instead of just going to the elevator and grabbing an escort, I'd opted for the stairs and told Rowan I'd see him in just a second. He was three feet away. Three feet. All I had to do was open the door, and he'd be there.

Instead, I was being dragged into darkness.

The hand loosened on my mouth, but before I could even gather a breath to scream, duct tape was slapped over my mouth. Zip ties secured my arms behind my back. I was so disoriented in the dark. And while freedom was still only three feet away, it might as well have been miles.

Stop feeling sorry for yourself and think. Think about it, Gwen. Where are you?

I was in Pendragon. This was my company, my home. So I had the benefit of knowing the building well. Or as well as I could for someone who had recently started. But since everyone in the building had been cleared, whoever was trying to take me couldn't know it as well as I did.

Chapter 26

I was on the fourteenth floor, just outside of my own hallway.

What's just outside that door?

Rowan. Safety.

Think.

Okay. Immediately, I tried to orient myself, and whoever grabbed me shuffled around. I tried to move, but I was connected to some kind of post.

Shit.

Something came up to my lips and I tried to avoid it, but hands grabbed at my hair, and they were gloved. Why were they gloved? Fingerprints, probably. But they were thick gloves, like winter weather gloves. Why wear those?

My abductor peeled the duct tape off my mouth sharply, causing micro tears on my lips, then something was pushed to my mouth again. It seemed like a thermos, but I didn't want it.

A hand tugged my hair back and poured the liquid into my mouth, which I immediately spat out, fearing they were trying to poison me. Whoever it was savagely released my head, shoving me forward and then the tape was back. Then I heard a rustling of clothes, and the door opened just enough for me to be aware of the brief wash of light. And then it was completely dark again.

And I was tied to a post.

How the fuck was I going to get out of this one?

27

ATTICUS

I had just gotten off my call and put my dick to sleep when Rowan came charging in. I expected to see Gwen right behind him as he'd been stationed on her floor. But his eyes were wide, and his lips set in a firm line. "Did Gwen leave?"

Those three little words sent me into a goddamn spiral.

"What do you mean, did Gwen leave?"

"Did Gwen fucking leave? She should have been downstairs ten minutes ago, but she never came down. She texted me right before she left your office. It should have taken her less than three minutes. I walked the whole floor in case she somehow went to the other elevator, but she knew where I always waited."

My heart stopped. I wasn't sure for how long, but it finally kicked into rhythm again, and all I could do was stare

Chapter 27

at him. The worst-case scenario had happened. My wife was gone.

I dragged in a sharp breath. "What do you mean?"

"We've lost the queen. We need everyone. Atticus, are you with me?"

I swallowed hard and nodded as my brain slowly charged up. Gwen. Gwen was gone.

It had happened. She had been here one second and was gone the next. She'd said she was on her way to see Jack.

"Jack. Did you find Jack?"

Rowan frowned. "No, why?"

"That's who she was meeting. Maybe he met her up here?"

He was on his walkie-talkie in seconds, telling everyone to hunt down Jack Farlow.

"We're searching floor by floor. Maybe she took the stairs instead of the elevator," Rowan suggested.

Oh, fuck.

I charged into the hallway, and the bile started to churn in my stomach as the voices in my head started to play games with me.

You took your eye off the ball. You thought you could play happy family. You didn't protect her enough. And now, someone has taken her.

Fuck. Fuck. Fuck. Where the fuck was she? I just needed her safe and sound and in my arms. I was never going to let her out of my sight again.

My body wanted to curl up and scream at the injustice. All she wanted was her freedom, and when I found her, I couldn't let her out of my sight.

Fuck.

Rowan stepped off the elevator and placed a hand on my shoulder. "Look, we'll find her. Just maybe go back to your office in case she comes back there."

I turned to stare up at him. "No. I should have made sure she got on the elevator."

"Atticus, we're doing a full sweep. I've got men on thirty, twenty, and ten, all working their way down."

"I'll just start from here, going down."

He nodded and handed me a security monitor panel before pointing out which screens to pay most attention to.

"These are blind spots right here, here, and here. Most essentially go to an office, and we have already checked all of those. She's not there, but we've got to look everywhere." Then he fixed me with a deep stare again. "We'll find her."

I nodded. I yanked open the door and started my hunt. I checked every fucking office, every conference room. Hell, I looked under a couple of desks. My executives stared at me. And when I stormed by Micah's office, I could see surprise, but I didn't stop. I was on a mission, and I did not have time to stop and chat.

Before long, I heard footsteps behind me and found my brother in my wake. "What's wrong?"

Chapter 27

"Gwen's gone. She left my office and told Rowan she was on her way down. And just like that, she was gone."

He stared at me. "Fuck. Give me something to do."

"Grab a security panel, I'm taking this floor then heading down to the next."

"Okay, I'll text Pierce. We're going to find her, Atticus."

And just like that, my brother was gone, also looking for her.

I hit the next floor, meticulously searching. And then next, which was our records floor, which just made me think of her. I checked every closet, every open panel. Anywhere that had space Gwen could squeeze into, I searched. Someone had grabbed her.

She couldn't have been taken out of the building. Rowan had already checked the exits. She was still on the premises, which meant someone was holding her somewhere.

As I searched, trying not to alarm my employees, my stomach churned. I had fucking lost her. I did not deserve her. It wasn't until I had searched my ten floors that Pierce's voice came over the walkie-talkie. "So far, we haven't found her. I searched through all the footage from the last hour, and she didn't leave the building. We need to put the building on lockdown."

My response was swift. "Lock it all down. No one gets out of this building. If someone has her, we're going to rip him to shreds. I'm getting my wife back today."

28

GWEN

My wrists were raw. How the hell was I going to get out of here?

Who the hell took me?

I tried to focus on anything that I remembered about the idiot who'd taken me as I tried to push myself to my feet. But all I'd heard were steps behind me. No voice, no nothing. My saving grace was that I was still in the Pendragon building. No one had come to take me out of the building, and we hadn't gone all the way downstairs. The bag over my head had served as more of a surprise tactic than a transportation tactic. So all I needed to do was get out of this damn utility closet before they came back for me.

I wasn't getting much sensory input in the dark, but I needed to figure out an escape plan.

Think Gwen, think.

Chapter 28

I knew my restraints weren't cuffs because there was no clanging, and plastic cuffs would have broken a lot easier by now with all my shifting, so it was definitely zip ties. But I had been left a little room to wiggle my wrists around.

What if they weren't trying to kill me, but scare me instead? It was a big mistake, because all they'd managed to do was piss me the fuck off.

On your feet.

I kicked off my boots, trying not to think about whatever the hell I was going to contract from the floor of whatever the hell closet I was in, and the cold concrete on my feet made me shiver. But slowly, I pushed to my feet, trying not to hyperextend my shoulders too much. I would need them in functioning order in just a second.

I managed to bend one knee and get it under the other and then pushed my weight forward as I shoved to my feet. Okay, I was standing. That was a success. My head still swam from whatever the hell I'd been given. Was that chloroform? Had I been injected? I was fighting for moments of awareness. I had to get clearheaded. I was in the building. Atticus would find me.

Atticus, God. He would be so terrified. And completely impossible to live with, because he would no longer let me out of his sight.

Which is fair.

I tested the pole I was against. It was a skinny pole. Probably some kind of water line?

Unfortunately, my hands had been secured behind my back, so no relatively easy zip tie escape. Morgan and I were into true crime and spent many hours watching videos on how to escape zip ties even though we would likely never be in that situation.

Never say never.

I had a little room, but not much. My brain tried to work out all the ways I knew of getting zip ties off. I tried raising my hands behind me, and bringing the force down behind the pole. I tried and tried, but my shoulders started to scream.

Come on, Atticus. Come for me.

And God, I hoped he'd fucking come for me before whoever had shoved me in here came back. What was the plan though? How did they plan to get me out of here? They were probably going to wait until the whole building was empty and then take me out through the service elevator or something. Somewhere there was a blind spot.

I winced again as I attempted to break myself lose, my shoulders screeching in pain. Fucking hell, this was going to require physical therapy again. I just knew it was. but I needed to free myself, regardless of the physical damage it might cause.

Something clanged behind me, and I frowned and then remembered they'd tied something around my mouth after they reapplied the duct tape. What was that? I just needed to get it off my damn mouth.

Chapter 28

I tried to twerk my body to reach the knot at my neck. With a series of pulls and tugs, I was able to unravel the knot.

Breathing heavily, I worked one end of the tie around the zip tie at my wrist. I wrapped it around, shoving my fingers, pulling and tugging, until I had it done once. And then I prayed to God I remembered how to do this correctly after only watching the YouTube video once.

I worked the other end of the tie and looped it around my other hand. With both hands together, I looped it back around. The next part would be the impossible part. On my tippy-toes, I raised my heels against the back of the pole and then pulled the tie and zip tie as taught as possible against my back. Dragging in several deep breaths, I tried to visualize myself, full weight forward. Visualize my hand coming loose. I bent all the way forward, bringing the zip tie taught against the pole as I tried to bring my face all the way down to my toes.

The problem was, I was not particularly stretchy. I really should have done more yoga. Atticus had said that along with the training for self-defense, they'd also work on my flexibility, saying that I would find it a whole lot of fun when he showed me how well he could use it in the bedroom.

Not that I didn't believe him, but the man was incorrigible.

The forward momentum helped me get my head down

further, and I tugged, pushing my heels against the pole and my frozen toes on the ground.

I tugged, and tugged, but all I could feel was a little bitty slip.

Think of Atticus, damn it. You are going home to see your husband. You are not going to sit here in the dark waiting for some psychopath to come and kill you.

Just thinking about Atticus's face and how much he would blame himself, thinking about how much he would hurt, made me tug harder. Thinking of my sister. Atticus would protect her. I knew he would. Atticus, and Micah, and Lance. They would all protect Morgan. The boys too. Pierce, and Gavin, and Sven, the lot of them. But she was *my* baby sister. No one could protect her better than me. Atticus would break. And I didn't want him breaking on my behalf. So, I needed to get the fuck out of these restraints.

With another grunt, I pulled forth with all the energy I could muster. And then suddenly, my full weight propelled me forward. I had barely a second to brace my hand in front of me before I landed forward on the concrete and hit my head.

But thank Christ, I was free.

I grabbed my wrist with the zip tie still attached and held it to my chest, massaging my shoulder. I was much better, but fucking hell did that hurt. My shoulders screamed, and physical therapy was going to be unpleasant this week.

I yanked the bag off my head and removed the duct tape

Chapter 28

from my mouth, but still had no light to see by. I bent down and felt around on the floor, finally locating and grabbing my boots. But instead of putting them on, I decided maybe it was better if I use them as weapons. I felt around for the door. When I turned the knob and ran out, the light blinded me, and I ran straight into a wall... of muscle.

29

ATTICUS

Heaven.

That was hiding behind door number two hundred and four. At least that's what it felt like. I had opened every damn door in this building myself, personally.

While Pierce, Rowan, Gavin, and Lance had continued to prowl over security cameras, talk to witnesses, and pull footage from across the street to make sure that Gwen hadn't, in fact, left the building in some way, I had opened every damn door, starting from the top floor down. And just like that, I opened the door to the utility room on the fourteenth floor, and out she spilled, right into my arms as if she had never left me.

My arms wrapped around her body, and I held her close as she shook. "I've got you, Gwen."

When the loud, racking sobs escaped her body, I only

Chapter 29

cuddled her tighter. "It's me, baby. I have you. Ness, you're safe now. I'm not letting you go."

She tried to pull back, but I couldn't let her go. All I could do was pull her tighter, eventually scooping her up and bracing my back against the wall as I held her and slid down, cuddling her to my body.

"I'm sorry. I'm so sorry. I should never have let you walk out of my office alone."

She didn't say anything. All she did was cry. Then the walkie-talkie went off, and Lance's strained voice said, "We have more footage, but none of it shows Gwen leaving the building."

I snapped out of it and realized everyone needed me to be tough. I picked it up and then pressed the button. "I have her. Repeat, I have her. Fourteenth floor, near the utility closet. Send the EMTs up."

She shook her head. "I don't need EMTs."

"I don't give a fuck what you think you need right now. This is what I need. I need you looked over from head to toe."

Lance's voice rang clear. "Over."

I dropped the walkie to cradle her face in my hands. "Baby, are you okay?"

Tears were streaming down her face, leaving tear tracks in the dirty smudges. "I-I... Physically, I think I'm fine. A little dizzy. They put a black bag over my head. And then—" She choked back a sob as a shudder racked her body.

I shook my head. "You don't have to talk about it. I have you. I was coming for you."

"And I was coming for you. I knew that you weren't going to survive if I stayed put and let them kill me. I was so scared, Atticus."

"I know. I was scared too. I'm so sorry, baby. I shouldn't have let you walk out of my office alone. Fuck."

She shook her head. "No, I-I think someone was waiting for me."

"What?"

"Yeah. It was almost as if someone knew that I liked to use the stairs, and that obviously, I spent a lot of time on your floor and mine. It was so easy. They just clocked me from behind, and they knew exactly where to stash me."

"Baby, it's okay. My lioness... You saved yourself. You didn't need me. I have been rendered obsolete." I tried for levity. Anything to quell my rising panic and hers. I had to make her feel okay. I hadn't been able to protect her. But now, I wasn't taking any of this for granted.

You haven't been. Sometimes bullshit happens.

I refused to acknowledge that. I refused to accept that bullshit just happened. I had to have some semblance of control, otherwise, what was the whole fucking point?

"Did he hurt you?"

She licked her busted lip. "I-I fell. I think I cut my head open when I hit the cement in there. But other than a kick to the abdomen, I'm okay, I think."

Chapter 29

"We're going to have you checked out, okay?"

I could hear the EMTs coming down the hall.

"Why didn't anyone hear you shout for help?"

"Because I was bound and gagged and only just now got the stupid gag off. I used it to help me get the zip ties off." She held up her wrists. One that was reddened and bruised, but free. The other, also red, but still bound by a zip tie.

"I'm going to fucking kill him."

"We have to find them first, Atticus. I'm scared. I'm so scared."

"Baby..." What could I say though? She *should* be scared. She absolutely should be. We weren't any closer to finding out who was trying to hurt her, and that motherfucker had gotten her in one of the places she should be absolutely safe. All I wanted to do was encapsulate her in bubble wrap and hide her somewhere safe like before.

"I really want to send you somewhere. A fucking fortress. But I won't do that to you again. If you go, I go too. We'd go together and tuck away, because I can't—" My voice broke, and I tucked her face to my chest once more. "I can't take the idea of something like this happening to you again. We'll run."

Gwen wriggled in my arms. "No. I'm not doing that again. If they want me, they can come and get me. Use me as bait. Whatever we need to do. I refuse to be scared for the rest of my life. You're my husband. I love you, and I want to be with you. But I refuse for us to be scared. I want a normal life. I want one where I can roam the stairwells of my own damn company and entice you to go get a smoothie with me. I want us to walk the streets without very large men following behind us, or in front of us for that matter. I want to just drive. I want to not worry about someone grabbing my sister to get to us. I want us to have a normal life, Atticus. I'm not hiding anymore. I'm done."

I heard her. I understood her. I knew why she wanted this, but what could I do? Every time I turned around, there was a new threat that I couldn't see clearly. "Right now, I'm not making any decisions, okay? Just let me hold you."

She lifted her head and met my gaze, her eyes stormy. "All I thought about was you. I'm not leaving you, I promise. They're going to have to take us both, because there is no way in hell I'm leaving without you either."

I held her tight. When I found out who was terrorizing us, I was going to kill them slowly as I watched their life leave their body, and I was going to enjoy it.

30

GWEN

I woke up alone in the dark. Panic flooded my veins immediately.

It took me several moments after sitting up to realize that I wasn't cold. There was no hard concrete beneath my ass. I was warm. In bed. I was safe.

The sliver of moonlight through the floor-to-ceiling windows told me I was at home with my husband. I curled into him, only to find that last statement to be untrue. I patted his side of the bed, finding it empty and cool.

What the fuck?

He hadn't pulled the covers taught like he normally did when he had left to work out or something. No, his side of the sheets were rumpled and a little bit damp. Was he sweating?

I quickly checked the bathroom, but there was no light

on, and he wasn't taking a shower. I grabbed the T-shirt that had long been discarded two hours ago when Atticus had thrown it somewhere over his head and proceeded to show me just how much he'd missed me. I dragged it over my naked body, but I didn't bother with underwear. I padded down the hallway and followed the light that was on in the kitchen.

And that was where I found him. On the floor of the pantry, his head in his hands, elbows on his knees, completely silent.

Quietly, I went to him and sat myself across from him, our toes touching. When he lifted his head, I saw the tears streaking down his face, and I wanted to hold him. I wanted to just reach over and grab him in my arms and tell him that it was okay, that I was okay, but I knew somehow that would be the wrong move.

"I don't know what to do," he choked out. "I can't fix this for you. I can't make it better. Everything I try ends in disaster. Someone is after you, and I can't even protect you. Maybe my father is right; I am a useless piece of shit. I keep trying to protect you, but all I do is put you in danger. We need to leave."

"Atticus, not this again. We're not leaving."

He clapped a hand to his chest. "Then tell me what to do, Gwen. This is my fault. We are in this predicament because of me. Whether it's my father, or Bronson, or someone else, they are coming after you because of me.

Chapter 30

Because I was unwilling to let you go. Because I chose you. Because they want revenge. And the easiest way to get to me is through you. I can't even keep you safe because I am unwilling to let you go again. If I was smart, I would have told Pierce to kidnap you and put you on a plane to Bumblefuck, Nowhere, and keep you there under lock and key. But I'm weak. I can't stand to be apart from you, and all I care about is your happiness and safety."

I knew he had to get this out, so I didn't bother interrupting and telling him that the only way Pierce was getting me on a plane without him was by killing me. I figured now was not the time for jokes. Not when he was this distraught.

"Everything I touch turns to shit. Just like my father fucking said."

This time, I scooted to him, intertwining our legs, and I took his hands. "Your father is a lying, narcissistic, sadistic user. That's it. That's all. He's not special. He's not magic. He's not powerful. We beat him. You, me, Micah, your mother, all of us together. We don't do anything apart. And I refuse to let you listen to that voice in your head. The one that he programmed. Seeing how Micah reacts to him and hearing the things he said to your brother just confirms he is the worst kind of human. But out of him, came the best thing in my life. You are good, and kind, and smart. You're shrewd and savvy, and you are *mine*. All mine. We're not running, Atticus. We do have to figure out some things, and maybe I need to stay home for a bit. Not because I'm hiding, but because we need a really good plan where I act as bait."

His brows immediately snapped down. "If you think—"

"That's just the thing, Atticus, either we let ourselves be controlled like your father controlled you your whole life, or we go on the offensive. But we're not going to talk about that right now. Right now, we're going to talk about why you're in here instead of in bed with me."

He rubbed the back of his hand over his nose. "I didn't want you to see me like this."

My heart broke in two. I had never seen him cry before. Not properly like this. Emotions fully out. I had never seen him let go enough.

"I messed up."

"You didn't mess up, Atticus. I should have just gone straight to Rowan. I should have been in the elevator. The point is, someone knew I took the stairs. That someone is the one at fault. And the next time you are worried, or scared, or upset, you come to me. You don't hide in the pantry, understand?."

"To be fair, I didn't intend to hide in the pantry. I came for Oreos."

I mock-gasped and clutched my hand to my chest. "All the sugar, Atticus, honestly."

He shrugged. "Dad would never let us have them. Whenever Micah or I were upset, Mom would sneak us a few. She kept them in her bedside table in the bottom

Chapter 30

drawer. Sometimes we would go in there and sneak a few ourselves. Our housekeeper at the time was sleeping with my father, so she told him everything going on around the house, and that's why Mom had to hide the cookies. Anyway, I came to see if we had any."

"I think we do. Have you ever put them over ice cream?"

"Isn't that just Oreo ice cream?"

I frowned. "Why on earth would you put them over vanilla?"

He shook his head, knowing exactly where I was going with this. "No, please don't tell me you put Oreo crumbles over other flavors."

"It's the best. Oreos over sherbet is chef's kiss."

He made a gagging sound, and I could see the hold the fear had on him dissipating slightly. Instead of dark, anguished storm clouds, it was more like the gray ones that maybe promised some rain, but not doom.

"Come on, I'll show you."

He shook his head. "No, I can't watch you eat something that disgusting. Maybe we'll just eat the Oreos."

"Okay. Just Oreos is good too. They're delicious. Oh, maybe Oreos and gummy bears. Hold on, I have a stash." I made to get up, but instead, he pulled me down onto his lap.

"That's okay. Maybe just stay here for a minute." I met his gaze, and his eyes searched mine. "I'm so sorry, Gwen."

"My life changed dramatically after meeting you on that balcony. That glitter-bombing was accidental, because I do not control the wind, but I like to think it was my mom giving me the love that I so desperately needed then. You brought nothing but good into my life, Atticus, whether you choose to see it that way or not. Now, it's you and me till death do us part. I mean, unless you're like super into me having one of those why-choose situations, in which case—"

He tugged me forward and planted a harsh kiss on my lips. "I'm the only choice you've got. Remember that."

"Oh, good. I'd rather not think about the extra dicks anyway. Just you and your very big—"

He kissed me again, more harshly, as if pouring every drop of emotion into the kiss and attempting to sear our souls together. When he pulled back, his eyes were clear. "I love you, Gwen."

"And I love you, Atticus."

"And just so you know, for the foreseeable future, you and I go nowhere without the other. I'm not going to keep you in prison, but wherever you are, I'll be there too. Because you're right; till death do us part. I'm not taking any more risks. You're my wife. And I'm your husband. Whatever we do, we do together."

31

GWEN

True to his word, Atticus hadn't gone all *me Tarzan, you Jane* on me.

But he had, very quietly, made sure that everywhere I went, he went.

Andrew had worked with my new assistant, Maya. I still had Carrie too, of course, but my new position as majority shareholder made the workload more than she could handle on her own. I turned up at work and there was Maya. She said she was there to make my life easier.

Honestly, it was very handy, because those smoothies Atticus liked to make me drink, she brought them to me.

She also brought one to him.

Because he was right there in my office. All the time. He had completely abandoned his. If he had a meeting, I joined him. And if I had a meeting, he joined me. He tried to give my team a little bit more privacy, because they would clam up if he was in their presence, but he was never more than ten feet away.

If I worked from home, he worked from home. It had been like this for a week.

He hadn't hired more people; he just made it a point that we were going to be together.

He also made it a point that under no circumstances was he going to revisit the conversation I had brought up after I had escaped. I *wanted* to be used as bait to draw out the person trying to kill me. But no. I'd even brought it up to Pierce and Gavin. Gavin laughed like I was insane. Pierce just shook his head, even though I could tell he thought it wasn't a bad idea.

"You're going to keep staring at him? It's disconcerting the way you two ogle each other."

I turn to Lance on the balcony of the penthouse. "What do you mean?"

"You are so aware of each other. And now every time you go out or you do anything, there he is, like a controlling boyfriend."

I frowned at him. "It's not like that."

"No, I know. I'm just saying it's odd. Never any time apart?"

"If I tell him I need a minute, he goes into another room. Not at work though. At work we are together."

Chapter 31

Lance shrugged and took a sip of his scotch. "I can't actually say I blame him for that one."

"Yeah."

"He was terrified, Gwen."

"I know. I just think that living like this is not going to work for the long term. He dragged me to work out with him yesterday. Me, working out. I mean, I love a good Pilates Reformer class, but his trainer is a masochist. There were weights involved."

Lance laughed. "There she is. There's my Gwen."

"Enough about this whole fucked up situation, which you hear about nonstop. Please, tell me something good."

He shifted on his feet and didn't look me in the eye. "I—I think I like someone."

Oh my God. "Fucking, at last. I mean look, I'm not thrilled about the age difference, but I think it's amazing that clearly you two have a thing, and I think that if you're careful and maybe just give her some time before you progress too far, it might actually really work out. Two people I love the most. I mean—" I'd been prattling on, but I realized that Lance was giving me a stricken look, and he just looked ill.

"What are you talking about?"

I frowned and glanced around. "What are *you* talking about? You and Morgan, right?"

He reared back as if I'd slapped him. "Morgan? No, that's disgusting. She's eighteen."

"Oh, come on. She'll be nineteen in a another month.

And like I said, she needs some time to have fun and be young and shit. But you're only twenty-six. It's not the end of the world. I mean, I don't think you two should move in together or anything like that yet, but if you want to date my sister and see if this insane chemistry thing that you have going on is for real, I'm down with it. I love both of you."

He shook his head vehemently. "No. She's just a kid, and I've known her since she was a *little* kid. That's—"

Shit. How the hell had I gotten that wrong? "Okay, sorry I brought it up. Clearly I was wrong."

"What's with you and Atticus?" he asked incredulously. "You should be looking out for Morgan. She needs someone her own age, some college guy who's worried about his internships. Not me."

"I'm sorry, Lance, but you have to see it. You are one of the smartest guys I know. You're telling me you do not see the Morgan thing?"

He shook his head. "I—No. Never going to happen. And you'll be happy to know I'm dating. There's a girl. A *woman*. Her name is Elia. It's newish, but she's appropriate. The right age. She's smart. And she—" He shook his head. "She's appropriate, Gwen. I need that."

I blinked slowly, sure I wasn't hearing that right. "Elia. You're for real?" For some reason, I couldn't see it. Was he serious? Who was this woman?

He nodded. "Yeah. I am. I need appropriate. Someone steady."

Chapter 31

I watched him warily, pretty sure I was being punked. "This Elia, what does she look like?"

"She's tall, with blond hair. Her mother's Scandinavian."

"Scandinavian," I parroted back. Every single girlfriend I'd ever known Lance to have had dark hair and was shorter and curvier, like my sister. Some tall, willowy blonde didn't seem like it fit. It took me a moment to realize he was still talking.

"And technically, Atticus wasn't your type either."

I rolled my eyes. "Atticus is *everyone's* type. You have eyeballs. That man is fine." But he had a point. I had tended to go for the guys who looked geekier and nerdier. The ones not encased in quite so much self-confidence.

You have to try harder. This is Lance, and he's excited. Be there. Support him.

"I'm sorry. I'm just surprised. You caught me off guard."

He shrugged. "It's all right. Yeah, so anyway, at some point, I'd like you to meet her. She's very interested in meeting you because I talk about you all the time."

Oh God. What had he said exactly? "Right. Of course. I'm so happy for you, Lance."

I threw my arms around him and hugged him tight, trying to let all the love I felt for him and his happiness really seep in. "I was just surprised. I thought you and..." I shook my head. "Never mind."

"No, it's fine."

"Big step for you."

He lifted a brow. "Be nice, Gwen."

"I *am* being nice. I am genuinely happy for you. You know that's all I've ever wanted."

He fixed me with his serious eyes. "And that's all *I've* ever wanted for you. You know that."

"Yeah. I know."

"You seem happy with Atticus, assassin notwithstanding."

I choked out a laugh. "Oh my God. For real?"

He laughed at that. "Only you would have an assassin on you and still be like, 'Oh, but I have to get this release out.'"

"Hey, I take work very seriously."

His laugh was so easy and familiar. "I know. But I'm glad that you are letting yourself enjoy life a little bit. That's all I ever wanted for you."

"Thanks. And when Elia comes, I will take her to lunch or something. Provided I'm allowed to leave the house by then."

"You'll be allowed to leave the house. I promise." He reached out and squeezed my hand. "This will all be over soon."

There was no way any of us could be sure of that. "We hope so. But last I checked, bestie, you are not clairvoyant."

"I may not be, but I have a hunch."

"Let's hope your hunches are right."

The door to the balcony busted open, and out came Morgan.

Chapter 31

"So this is where you two are hiding."

I must have made a funny face at her, because she hesitated before rushing to explain. "I swear, whatever Lance said I did, I didn't. It's not my fault. He was bad at teaching me how to drive clutch."

What on earth? I frowned at Lance. "You were teaching Morgan to drive clutch?"

He shifted on his feet. "It's stupid that she doesn't know how. In case of emergency, she should always have a way out of a situation."

She rolled her eyes. "I stripped his clutch, and now he's mad at me."

I watched as the muscle in his jaw ticked. "No, I'm pissed at you because you called the goddamn Maserati pretentious then proceeded to drive it like you were Hamilton with Verstappen on his ass."

My sister shrugged. "Well, I mean, I tried. Maybe if you weren't yelling all the time."

I winced and backed up as I watched the two of them. From zero to sixty in two seconds. How the hell could he not see that the two of them were a match made in, well, not quite heaven. But they had so much tension, and their chemistry was off the charts.

He was right that Morgan was young. And to me Lance was just Lance, but he was older. But when I saw the way they reacted to each other, my brain just said, *Oh God, get a room.* I knew my mind had gone on a little vacay when the next words I heard were, "God, you are such a pain in the ass. It's no wonder you don't have a girlfriend."

"Well, I do, as a matter of fact, and she's coming here in two weeks. Hell, I might even make her my fiancée."

And *that's* when I tuned back in.

My gaze darted to Morgan's, and I watched as her face fell. Witnessing someone else's heartbreak was beyond painful.

But she was my sister. She was strong and tried to recover. "Oh God, I feel sorry for her. Well, at least you won't be a menace to the women of New York any longer."

When I looked at Lance, there was something in his expression. Worry? Sadness? Regret? "When she arrives, you can meet her."

"Oh my God, yes. I can't wait to meet her," Morgan said, sarcasm dripping from every word. "Hopefully she will not be as insufferable as you are."

And with that, my sister turned and headed back inside. One glance at Lance told me he was going back to the scotch.

"So what the fuck was that Lance?"

His gaze darted to mine and then away quickly. "That was me shutting a door."

32

ATTICUS

I checked the security monitor for the fifth time just to make sure Gwen was okay while she visited with Lakewood. I had a meeting that couldn't be put off, so I'd come in for it, and Micah had made me stay for a drink.

"You know, I'm impressed with you not losing your shit."

I lifted a brow. Had I gotten that good at masking? "I am. But that's not what Gwen needs right now. She needs me calm and present. So I'm thinking about some kind of sabbatical, just the two of us, and getting her out of here."

My brother watched me surreptitiously from the corner of his eye. "You seem very calm."

I shrugged. "I am. I know what to do now. Before I didn't know what to do. I couldn't fix it."

My brother's sighed. "You know I love you, right?"

I smirked at him. "Yes, Merlin. Drop your wisdom on me."

He gave me a knowing smile and nodded. "My liege."

"You can feel free to call me King Arthur if you like," I said with a smirk.

My brother rolled his eyes. "No chance. But seriously, I *do* love you."

I shrugged. "Yeah, I know." It wasn't the norm for Micah to openly express his feelings. He did it from time to time, but usually he was an actions kind of guy.

"So I want you to hear me where I'm coming from, but this is bullshit. You're scared, and you have given up. I can see the toll it's taking on you. You realize you haven't left your wife alone in ten days, right? Like, from where we're sitting right now, enjoying our very fine Lagaluvin, you can see her from here."

What the hell was his point? "It works better this way. You don't know what it's like for the person you love to just... Poof."

He shifted in his seat. "Maybe I don't know that kind of pain. But I love her like a sister, so I did feel it. I mean, I don't love her like *you* love her, but I love you both, and it hurts."

"Right? Then you should understand."

"I understand the *compulsion*. But because I love her too, I can see you're about to start smothering her."

The fuck? "She understands. She doesn't mind."

"I know she doesn't *mind*, but at some point she's going to

Chapter 32

want to use the bathroom without having to check in with you. At some point, she's going to want to get fresh air without you. It's a mark of a healthy relationship. Her ability to be on her own. Your ability to be on your own."

"I know what healthy looks like. I am currently not there." But someone tried to take her from me. What the fuck else was I supposed to do? She already didn't want me murdering anyone.

"That's what I'm saying. Look at how tense you are."

"That's because someone *tried to kill my fucking wife*," I ground out through clenched teeth.

"I know. It's not fair, and it's not right. But if you start trying to chain her to your side, you are going to smother the light that is her. The very bits that you loved about Gwen, from her glitter bomb, to that bright-ass smile, to her obsession with gummy bears, for the love of Christ. You're going to steal all of that light if you keep doing this."

My heart squeezed at that. "What am I supposed to do, Micah?" I drained my glass, the burn constricting my throat as it slipped down my esophagus and into my belly.

"Love her and understand what *she's* going through. I mean, I know what *you're* going through. I've seen it. But imagine her being scared all the time, needing to look over her shoulder only to find that her husband is right there. You know that meme on social media, the one about every time a woman is enjoying herself, there's a man in the corner all in her business?"

I frowned. "No."

He shrugged. "Whatever. You get the idea."

I watched her with Lakewood. Morgan had joined them out on the balcony, and of course, Lakewood and Morgan were having their tense little situation.

"You see that shit with Lakewood? What's up with him?"

Micah chuckled. "I don't know, but I caught him on the phone earlier, and he was using that *I'm trying to get some* voice."

"Ew." A shudder racked my body.

My brother laughed. "A tender one, like the kind of voice you use with Gwen."

"Well, I use *all* the good voices with Gwen."

This time Micah shuddered. "Oh God, you're going to make me gag."

"Are you sure it wasn't Morgan he was talking to?" I asked.

He pointed at the three of them on the balcony. "Does that look like he's speaking to her softly?"

"Yeah, good point," I conceded. "How long do you think it's going to take for him to realize that he's into her?"

Micah shrugged. "He probably won't know until it's too late."

"Oh, fantastic. And then of course he's going to need to talk to Gwen about it."

He laughed. "I see you're getting used to him."

"I'll admit he's come in handy."

Chapter 32

My brother smirked at me. "Right. Handy. You like him."

"I do *not*."

"If you say so," he teased.

"I *do* say so."

"Look, just think about what I said and figure out the best way to ease up on Gwen, okay? Because I know you're scared. I've seen this look on your face before when you were desperate to protect your mom. And obviously, I understand it. I am desperate to protect her too, but not like this. You have to talk to her. And keep talking to her. Listen to her. Because she may have an idea about all this that you're not willing to listen to."

I narrowed my eyes at my brother. "Oh, for fuck's sake. She brought up the using-her-as-bait thing to you too?"

Micah shrugged. "It's not the worst idea we've ever heard, and it expedites this bullshit. At least we'd draw whoever it is out in the open."

"We are not putting her at risk. I'm not going to have it."

"That's what I told her. I'm just saying that discussing it might be a good idea."

"Yeah, whatever."

"Mate," he said impatiently, "she just really needs you to love her. That's all. She doesn't need a protector. You've got hired men for that. You need to give her what *she* needs, not what you need."

"Is that what all your books say?"

"Well, most of my books just say to growl at her a lot and

say filthy things. But somewhere there is always a revelation of feelings, and listening, and communication, and all that shit."

"Right, maybe I'll start with the growling thing."

"Oh of course, that's where you'll start. Just growl that you love her then start listening."

I watched her laugh at something Lakewood said, and then she dropped an arm around her sister's shoulders, tugging her in tight. Then suddenly, Morgan charged back inside, and she looked pissed.

As I watched my wife, I wondered how much of what Micah said was true. All I wanted to do was protect her, but maybe I needed to let her fight.

33

GWEN

Someone must have said something to Atticus. If I had to guess, it was either Micah or Lance. Because that morning, he woke up, kissed me on the lips, and told me he was giving me a day to myself. It had been almost two weeks of him hovering. Sweetly hovering. Making the kind of love to me that I was pretty sure only happened in Micah's romance novels, often three times a day. It was how I woke up. It was how I went to bed, and when we worked from home, lunch consisted of me first. I was not complaining. But it was nice to finally have silence in the house. It was hard to feel like he wasn't constantly worrying or looking over my shoulder.

Before he left though, he left me specific instructions for the panic room and told me that Sven and Rowan were just down the hall in the other penthouse.

He'd rented it out just for my safety. The old flat that I'd been using while we were hiding our marriage from his father was too far away. I made a face about the cost, but Atticus did not care. "What good is money if I can't use it for what we need?"

Anyway, when I finally woke up for good around seven-thirty, I took my bodyguards with me for a workout in the gym. Sven used the time for more self-defense training.

"So unnecessary, Sven."

"No, it's not. You've already needed it once." He said it with a grim face lined with worry, like an older brother. I had no idea how old Sven was. With his short hair and his naturally craggy face, it was hard to tell. Sven did not take it easy on me at all. He showed me how to escape from a choke hold, how to escape an attacker trying to grab me from behind, and how to slip from an attacker trying to grab my arms. Quick lessons on how to breathe, so I didn't panic and I could think.

When I got back to the penthouse, I heard bustling in the kitchen, and I called out before I headed down the hall to grab a shower. "Magda, don't bother with a smoothie. There's this new scone place down the block, and I think I'm going to grab one from there. Do you want me to get you one after I shower?"

She didn't respond, so I rounded the corner. I could hear humming in the kitchen, figuring she probably had her earbuds in.

But when I turned left instead of right to let her know I

Chapter 33

was home, it wasn't Magda who smiled at me. "Ah, Gwen darling, there you are."

My eyes went wide, and my gaze flickered around. "What are you doing here, Lucy?"

She grinned. "Well, I saw Magda at the service entrance when I was parking my car. Obviously, Magda and I are friends, so she let me up. Isn't that sweet?"

I started backing up. Could I make it to the panic room?

You're being paranoid. Maybe Lucy is looking for Morgan.

"Right. Well, I don't think Morgan's here. She has classes this morning."

She frowned. "Are you sure? She told me to come this morning."

"Yeah, she's got classes all day. Her schedule is right there on the refrigerator. Where's Magda?"

"Oh, she wanted to have a lie down. She'd done some shopping, so I helped her bring it in." She indicated one of the bags on the counter, and I recognized the label from one of the stalls at the Farmers' Market down the street that we liked to go to.

"Right. So she must have told you already that Morgan is not here," I said as I started to back up.

As I retreated, Lucy advanced. "You know, she might have mentioned it. But I figured since you're almost always here, you and I could talk."

"I'm not sure what you want to talk about."

Fuck. Fuck. Fuck. Fuck.

And no Atticus today. Fucking hell. How on earth had this happened?

My brain tried to work it all out. Was it Lucy trying to kill me? But that wouldn't make any sense. Lucy didn't know how to shoot anyone. She was a socialite.

But still, every instinct in my body told me to run. To head down to the panic room and lock myself in. Atticus had told me to listen to my instincts, so I inched to the left.

Lucy took another step toward me. "You see, you and I have so much in common, you know? You're fucking my man."

"I beg your pardon?" That made me halt. "You and Atticus have been over for a long time now."

"Yeah, about that. We haven't been. We have been sleeping together this entire time. He only married you because of that deal with your father."

For one brief, horrifying moment, the axis of my world tilted. After all, Lucy was the right fit for him. She was a socialite. The right kind of socialite. Blond, refined, what people expected. He'd never have to explain to anyone how or why *she* was his wife. They'd never have to endure the double takes and the questioning looks because she fit what people expected of him.

But just as the thought started to take hold, I looked at her. *Really* looked at the gleam in her eye, and I knew she was lying.

Chapter 33

I pretended to sob and clutch my chest for one second, and then I took off running. I was faster and stronger than she was, so I didn't even pay attention to the thumping feet behind me. I just kept running. Twenty feet. Fifteen. Ten.

And then pain flashed along my back, right at the same shoulder the bullet had struck. And my brain went fuzzy as a wave of dizziness took me.

I screamed, clutching my shoulder as I continued to try and run, but that stab had caused me precious moments, and she was on me then.

She kicked me, and I went sprawling to the floor. She climbed on top of me, wrenching the knife out of my shoulder for a second of blessed relief. But I knew if I stayed like that, she was going to stab me in the back. Literally.

I forced in a deep breath, just like Sven had taught me. Deep in, short one out. I tightened every muscle in my body then did what he'd taught me, drawing elbows to knees and bucking her off me.

Once she was off and went sprawling before me, I grabbed the knife that she'd lost and cast it behind me somewhere. If she wanted to fight me, she was going to have to fight me unarmed.

I screamed, "Avalon, Avalon!" That was the code word, and I prayed to God the guys could hear me next door. "Avalon! Avalon!"

Meanwhile, Lucy launched herself at me again, aiming for my face. But I ducked and tucked my shoulders straight into her ribs, sending her sprawling back again and landing on top of her.

She thumped at my back to no avail, but then she had better success because she grabbed at my ponytail, yanking my head back, and I had no choice but to release her. I staggered backward, and then she punched me in the throat.

And there went my fight. I couldn't breathe. I grasped at my throat as if I could claw the air in there myself.

Then she punched me in the gut and launched herself at me again, hitting me with an elbow. And when I fell backward, barely able to brace my fall, she dug her elbow into my shoulder and grinned down at me.

"You stupid bitch. Why won't you just die? When I had Reeser shoot you, I thought that would be it. I thought for sure you were going to die. But oh no, because you have the luck of the Irish themselves, you didn't die. And there was Atticus, proclaiming his love for you all over the place. I saw him on the news. He was worried. He used to love me like that, you know?"

I could barely breathe, only getting a little of my air back. And this time, she levered herself up and then bounced on my sternum, sending out whatever air I'd managed to take in. But still, I croaked out, "He never loved you."

I groaned and tried to dislodge her again. But her delicate hands were on my throat as she attempted to squeeze the life out of me. "Lying cunt. He did love me. You just got in the way and distracted him. I've been told about girls like

Chapter 33

you my whole life. The ones that the boys shouldn't want but can't help themselves. You are nothing but a whore. I thought he would get over it like they're supposed to. I am the proper wife. *Me.* Not someone like you."

She pulled me up and then smashed my head back into the tile floor. My mind went fuzzy for a moment. Then I tried to raise my arms up over my head like Sven had taught me to draw in a longer breath. I made C-shapes with my hands and brought them down right at her thumb, and dragged in a breath. With that, I raised my hips and rolled her over. Finally, I was back on top, and I delivered an elbow to her face. She screeched. "Fuck you."

I shouted again, "Avalon." And I kept shouting the code word as I delivered blows to her face then began choking her.

But she had some skill, and she was able to dislodge me, kicking me against the wall, making me bang my head again. And then she scrambled for the knife. I only had seconds before she reached it. Staggering, I ran toward her and shoved her down.

"Avalon!"

I grabbed the back of her hair, hard, and then smashed her head down into the tile floor. "Avalon!"

No one was coming. I was on my own. I was going to have to incapacitate her if I wanted to make it to the panic room.

Suddenly, Lucy was tugging for something inside her belt at the small of her back.

"You stupid bitch. You are going to die today. I wanted to carve off your pretty face first, but I'm happy to shoot you just the same."

When I realized she had a gun in her hand, I fought for it.

One shot rang clearly in the penthouse, and my breath caught.

I am not going to die today. I am not going to die today. I am not going to die today.

At that point, I was able to bang the gun against the floor and kick it away.

She scrambled for it, and I ran after her.

Then suddenly, Atticus was there. He was coming through the door in the kitchen. The one that connected the two penthouses.

And as Lucy raised her gun, he ran in front of me. "That's enough, Lucy."

"No, that isn't enough."

Behind him, I sagged, but I wasn't going to let him take a bullet for me. Instead, I stepped to the side.

"I said, that's enough," he repeated.

"You should have chosen me, Atticus. We were perfect together, but instead, you threw me away."

Atticus raised an insolent brow. "Correct me if I'm wrong, but didn't you fuck Jefferson behind my back?"

Chapter 33

Her eyes went wide and her mouth hung open. "No. When I was with you, I was with you."

"That's why I broke up with you. If you want to fuck some McKinsey reject, fine, I don't care. But I'm not going to be with someone who likes to fuck other people. It was that simple."

Lucy's eyes narrowed to slits. "You married a slut."

Atticus's voice was sharp when he spoke again. "You will not talk about my wife like that."

"You should have fallen for me, but I'm going to make the choice for you. When she's gone, you'll learn to love me again like you did before. You and me, we're supposed to be together. You know how good we look. You look wrong with her. With her skin and her hair, she doesn't fit, Atticus."

"I said that's fucking enough, Lucy!"

He shifted his weight so that he was in front of me again.

Lucy just droned on and on. "Everything was perfect before her. You would have come back. How can you choose someone like her instead of me? *I'm* the damn prize, not someone like her, Atticus. You're just confused. I know what you've heard about women like her. And I get it. It's exciting. But you've slummed it long enough. Come back to me now."

Slummed it? I'd heard quite enough at that point. "What the hell? Just who do you think—"

Atticus would not let me step out from behind him to bitch slap her. "Like I said, you will not disrespect my wife. You're done here, Lucy."

Suddenly, the others were running through the door. Pierce, Micah, Gavin, Rowan. And all of them except Micah had guns pointed at Lucy.

She swung her gun around. "I swear to God, I might die, but I will kill every single one of you. I don't care as long as I kill her."

Atticus shook his head, taking yet another step in front of me. This time, walking toward her. "You're not going to kill Gwen. You're going to put the gun down. You've had enough. You made your bed when you hired an assassin to kill my wife."

Micah's voice was a warning. "Atticus, no."

But he kept walking toward her. "You tried to kill her, and then hired someone else when you couldn't get the job done."

"He kept missing. She was with you all the time. Can't you see she's useless?"

"You tried to take the only person who has ever understood me. *You* tried to take that from me," Atticus said with gravel in his voice. "You think I could be with anyone who was like that?"

"I understand you. I do. You just never gave me a chance."

He took another step toward her. "Oh, I gave you a chance. I gave you a million chances. Even if Gwen wasn't here, I would never ever be with you in a million years. Not to mention, I would hate you for takin her from me."

Chapter 33

Her brows furrowed. "But you love me, Atticus."

"Even when I was with you, I never loved you. Gwen's the only woman I've ever loved. Get that through your thick skull, Lucy."

He was right in front of her.

Micah shifted next to me, placing his body slightly in front of mine now that Atticus was no longer shielding me. And then so quickly that I couldn't even see it, Atticus whipped his hand out, grabbed her wrist, bent it back and then forward, releasing the gun from her hand.

Then his hands went to her throat.

"Atticus, no," I screamed. "No! Not for me. I know who you are. This isn't you."

"She was going to kill you, Gwen."

"I know. But you saved me. It's over."

Sidestepping Micah, I walked up to him. I kicked the gun even further out of the way. Gavin went around and grabbed it off the floor and tucked it at the back of his trousers. Then I put my hand on Atticus's back, rubbing gently. "I'm okay. We have to go and check on Magda."

Sven's voice was low as he spoke from behind me. "Fuck, I'll check on Magda."

I kept my gaze on Atticus and the way he was squeezing her neck. "Look at me. Atticus, look at me, here."

His gaze flickered to mine briefly before landing back on Lucy.

"Atticus Price, you look at me right now."

His gaze slid back to me, and I gave him a soft smile. "I thought I was the only one you choked."

And just like that, the spell was broken, and he was no longer that version of himself I didn't know.

He released her quickly, and a laugh tore out of his chest on a choked sound. The moment he released her, Pierce and Rowan came forward, grabbing her.

She tried to claw at them as she reached for Atticus. "No, let him do it. Let him kill me. If he kills me, he goes to jail. And then he can't have her anyway, which is perfect."

But they were already taking her away.

I grinned at her. "Sweetheart, the whole penthouse is wired with cameras. Do you really think he would go to jail after what you tried here? Never."

She continued to claw at Pierce and Rowan as they dragged her through the vestibule. Rowan was securing zip ties around her wrists as she bucked in his arms.

"Hold up," I shouted. The men stopped, and Atticus tried to pull me back, but I wiggled out of his grasp. They turned Lucy toward me, and I looked her up and down. "You are despicable."

When she spat in my face, I laughed. "Okay, you're going to enjoy jail." I turned slightly and rotated my hips just like Sven had taught me before I released a punch straight to her nose.

This time, Atticus reached for me. "Gwen..."

"That's for using my sister, you bitch."

Chapter 33

Atticus tucked me to his chest. "Oh my God, I fucking love you, but you're also insane."

"I know." I winced as I tried to curl my hand into a fist. "I hope that hurt."

The guys finally got her in the elevator, taking her down, presumably to the police, or to kill her and bury her body. I didn't really care which.

Atticus eased me away from them. "Are you okay?"

"I have a hell of a headache."

"I'm so sorry. I got here as fast as I could. I'm so sorry."

"I thought you were in the office today."

He winced. "Well, I didn't want to be that far away from you, so I rented one of the offices on the fourth floor too."

"You—" I shook my head. "Of course you did."

"Sorry, but there was no way I'd go all the way to the office and just leave you here."

"You know what? Today, I'm glad for your clingy ways."

"Good. I should have been here sooner. Pierce ran in, having identified who the assassin had been in contact with. But we had to take the stairs. She used an electronic device to disable the elevator."

I held him tightly to me and buried my face in his chest, knowing I was getting him bloody but not caring. "It's over. It's finally over."

"Yeah, it is. The authorities have already picked up Peter Reeser. You're safe. Nothing is ever going to hurt you again."

34

GWEN

"Look at us," Morgan giggled. "Sitting outside and everything."

I nodded at my sister. "Yes, and not a single hulking bodyguard to be found."

Atticus frowned. "Don't worry, Sven is still here somewhere."

As we sat on the balcony of La Table Ronde, I felt relaxed for the first time in months.

Reeser had, in fact, been arrested. Lucy had been too, and they were doing a psychological evaluation on her. My cuts and bruises on my shoulder were healing, but my physical therapist was pissed.

Everything worked out exactly like it was supposed to.

Lance was looking antsy, rubbing his hands on his thighs and checking the door. Morgan narrowed her eyes at him,

Chapter 34

but that was normal. Ever since that night on the balcony, the two of them had been even weirder than usual. It was odd, though. They fought a lot less, but now it felt like two people who really hated each other. Which made me sad. Maybe it was my fault for suggesting that there was something there.

Atticus sat forward, his smile bright. He smiled a lot easier now. What a difference a few months made. That was my smile. The one he usually reserved for me, but he was using it on my sister now. "So, Morgan, what are we doing for your birthday?"

Micah piped up then. "Ooh, yes, there's a book signing. That author you like who writes about the dragon shifters, she's going to be there. We can get tickets if you want to go."

She wrinkled her nose. "But isn't it in Dallas? I don't want to go to Texas on my birthday."

"Fair," Atticus said, giving Micah a withering look. "Where do you want to go?"

"Somewhere with really big fucking roller coasters."

Lance's gaze turned to her. "Roller coasters? Really, Morgan?"

Morgan grinned at him. "Yes, roller coasters. I figured it is my last year as essentially a kid. One more year, and I'll be in my twenties, a proper adult. This birthday might be the last time I get to do a kid thing."

I shook my head. "You can do kid things for as long as

you want. Did you not see Atticus last night, losing his shit over getting crushed at Monopoly?"

Atticus sat back and glowered at me, and I knew that remark would earn me a spanking later. "That's because you were cheating."

I stuck my tongue out at him. "Prove it."

"I have something for you to do with that tongue."

Immediately, Gavin, Rowan, Micah... Well, basically everyone at the table made gagging noises.

"Oh, I bet you do." I grinned. "But not until you apologize for the shitty response to losing."

"I didn't lose," he grumbled

God, I loved antagonizing him. It was so much fun.

He made to push his chair back. "If you'll all excuse me, I think I need to have a quiet conversation with my wife."

"And by conversation, you mean a shag in the bathroom?" Morgan asked. "Because ewww..."

I couldn't help but laugh. This was what it felt like to be relaxed, have a family, and enjoy ourselves.

I glanced around, reveling in it.

Atticus turned his attention back to my little sister. "Let's have it, little sis. What do you really want to do?"

"I think I really do want to do roller coasters. And I want everyone there. Bring your partners, bring your kids. Gavin, I can't wait to meet your daughter."

He grinned. "You will be her favorite person for suggesting an amusement park."

Chapter 34

Pierce was the only one frowning. "I don't know if I like the security logistics for that."

Atticus just laughed. "Oh, Jesus. Look, I'll buy out the place for a day or two. Morgan, which one do you want?"

My sister laughed nervously. "What?"

"Which amusement park do you want? Do you want like a Universal? A Disney property is going to be a bit pricey, but we can do it. Or do you want like a Six Flags? You really need to be certain about the kinds of roller coasters you want to ride."

My sister's gaze nervously skittered between me and Atticus, and even at Lance a time or two for some help. "What do you mean by pricey?"

My husband just shrugged. "I mean, it's your birthday, so we'll just buy it out. You can ride anything you want as often as you want. And you can even make Lance your ride partner."

Lance definitely looked gray at that. "I will not be her ride partner."

Morgan just laughed evilly. "Oh yes, you will. It's my birthday. I get to have whatever I want."

He just shifted uncomfortably in his seat. Lance had always hated roller coasters. He couldn't even do fair rides. The Ferris Wheel made him very nervous. And he *could* just tell her that, but he wouldn't. Because whatever weirdness was going on with them now, he would never admit defeat to

Morgan. "Fine, pick your poison. I bet you give up long before I do."

Atticus gave me that soft, elusive, corner-of-his-lip smile, which told me he was getting exactly what he wanted. "Fantastic. You just have to pick the best location. How about Universal in Los Angeles?"

I grinned at that. "Yeah. That way we'll get great dinner options, get to do some shopping on Rodeo Drive, and do touristy shit like visit studios."

Morgan clapped her hands together. "I love it. But you don't have to shut down Universal Studios for me."

Atticus shrugged. "I'm doing it for Micah. With his delicate sensibilities, he couldn't possibly wait in line."

I tossed a bottle of sunscreen at my husband, who, shockingly, caught it adeptly. "I'm pretty sure it's Atticus who won't wait in line. He is never very patient."

As everyone chatted, my sister leaned over to me. "He's not really going to rent out Universal Studios, is he?"

"Oh, he most definitely is. You've met him, right?"

"I don't want all that. Especially since all of this was my fault." She dropped her gaze as if ashamed. "I feel terrible about bringing Lucy into the apartment."

I took my sister's hand and squeezed it. "That was not your fault. Remember, we lay blame at the feet of those who perpetrated injustice, not anywhere else."

"I know, but I don't want to be rewarded for being a dumbass."

Chapter 34

"You're being rewarded because it's your birthday, and you deserve to celebrate. Enjoy it. Besides, you know full well you can't tell Atticus anything. He does as he pleases."

"Or rather, he does as you please."

The hem of my skirt shifted under the table. My gaze flickered to my husband, who grinned at me and winked.

I just ignored him. We'd already been late coming to brunch because of him. He'd taken one look at my sundress, and before I could protest, he had me bent over the couch and moaning.

When his fingers teased higher up my thigh, I grabbed his hand and shook my head, which only made him pout.

At the end of the table, I saw Lance spring up and walk back into the restaurant. When he rejoined us, he gave me a big smile. "What did I miss?"

Atticus took my hand. "You're just in time for me to ask Gwen to marry me again."

35

ATTICUS

I HAD PLANNED the day down to the last detail. Cake tasting —because of course Gwen's stepmother insisted on handling every aspect of our second wedding, which meant that we had to endure the mind-numbing rituals of planning it. But I didn't mind so much. At least it was something we could do together, something that didn't involve security protocols or me watching her every move like a hawk.

But Gwen was acting off. As I watched her pick at her breakfast, her brow furrowed in concentration, I could tell something was wrong. She was normally excited about anything involving food, especially cake. Yet here she was, pushing a piece of toast around her plate as if it might bite her.

"Not hungry?" I asked, trying to sound casual.

Chapter 35

She shook her head, frowning at the toast like it had offended her. "I don't know. Everything just smells weird."

"Weird how?" I set my coffee down and studied her. She looked pale, and there was a slight crease between her brows, a sign that she was in discomfort.

"Like... fish. I swear everything smells like fish." She wrinkled her nose in disgust and pushed her plate away. "And why does your cologne smell so strong today? Did you put on extra?"

I blinked, thrown by the sudden shift. "It's the same as always, Gwen."

She sighed and rubbed her temples. "Maybe it's just me. I don't know what's going on. The whole penthouse smells off too. And this décor, what was I thinking? It's all wrong. I can't stand looking at it."

I frowned. Gwen had meticulously chosen every single item in this penthouse, down to the last throw pillow. She'd been proud of her choices, confident in her style. To hear her suddenly despise it was... unusual. More than that, it was alarming.

"Maybe you're coming down with something," I suggested, keeping my tone neutral even as a spike of worry shot through me. I didn't like seeing her like this—confused, upset, and uncomfortable. "We can skip the cake tasting. You should stay home and rest."

"No," she said, her voice firm despite the unease in her

eyes. "I'm not missing this. Clarissa and Morgan would never let me hear the end of it if I did. Besides, I'll be fine."

But she didn't *look* fine. She looked pale and a little... off. And when her eyes suddenly filled with tears, my heart nearly stopped.

Gwen *never* cried. Not over something like this. Something was seriously wrong.

I reached out, my hand hovering uncertainly over hers before I finally set it down gently. "Gwen, talk to me. What's really going on?"

She looked up at me, her eyes shimmering with unshed tears, and for the first time in a long time, I felt completely helpless. "I don't know," she whispered. "I just feel... off. Everything feels wrong, and I can't explain it."

Seeing her like this was like a punch to the gut. Gwen was always so strong, so put together. And here she was, unraveling right in front of me, and I had no idea how to fix it.

"I'll be right back," I said abruptly, my mind racing as I stood up. Something was gnawing at the back of my brain, a thought that I hadn't dared to entertain until now. I had to know for sure.

She blinked up at me, confused. "Where are you going?"

"I just need to check something. I'll be back in a few minutes. Stay here, okay?"

Before she could protest, I was out the door, panic

Chapter 35

clawing at my insides. As soon as I was in the elevator, I pulled out my phone and dialed Micah.

He answered on the second ring. "What's up, brother?"

"I need a favor," I said, my voice tight. "I need you to meet me downstairs. Now."

Micah didn't ask questions. He knew me well enough to understand when I was serious. "On my way."

I was pacing the lobby when he arrived, his brow furrowed in concern. "What's going on?"

I didn't have time for explanations. "I need you to go to the pharmacy and buy as many pregnancy tests as you can get your hands on. All different brands. Whatever they have."

His eyes widened in surprise, but to his credit, he didn't question me. "Got it. I'll be back in ten."

Those ten minutes felt like an eternity. I kept replaying everything in my head—Gwen's sudden aversion to smells, her nausea, the way she was reacting to the décor she had once loved. Could it be...?

Micah returned with a bag full of boxes and handed it to me. "You're sure about this?"

"No," I admitted, taking the bag from him. "But I need to know."

He gave me a long, considering look before nodding. "Good luck."

When I returned to the penthouse, Gwen was curled up on the couch, fast asleep. She looked so peaceful, and for a moment, I hesitated. But I needed to know. I needed to be sure.

I set the bag down gently on the couch beside her and knelt down, brushing a strand of hair away from her face. "Gwen, wake up."

She stirred, her eyes fluttering open. "Atticus? What's going on?"

I swallowed hard, my heart pounding in my chest. "I need you to pee on all of these."

Her eyes widened in confusion as she sat up, looking at the bag. "What? Why?"

"Just... humor me, okay?"

She stared at me for a long moment, clearly trying to make sense of what I was asking. Then, slowly, realization dawned. "Atticus, are you serious?"

I nodded, my throat too tight to speak.

She looked at the bag again, her expression somewhere between shock and amusement. "There's not enough pee in the world for that."

"Try," I said, my voice almost pleading. I needed to know. I needed her to tell me that what I was thinking wasn't just a wild fantasy.

Gwen's lips quirked into a small smile, and for the first time all morning, I saw a glimpse of the woman I knew. "You really think...?"

"I don't know," I admitted, running a hand through my hair. "But if you are, I need to know. Please, Gwen."

Chapter 35

She stared at me for a long moment, and then she nodded, her smile widening just a fraction. "Okay. Let's do this."

As she took the bag from me and headed toward the bathroom, I stood there, my heart in my throat, my mind racing with possibilities. And for the first time in weeks, I felt something other than fear or guilt.

Hope.

It was a fragile, tentative hope, but it was there, and I clung to it with everything I had.

Whatever happened next, we would face it together. And that thought, more than anything, gave me the strength to breathe again.

EPILOGUE
MORGAN

The reception was in full swing, fairy lights twinkling above us like stars. The New York Public Library had been transformed into a wedding wonderland, every inch of it dripping with opulence.

Crystal chandeliers hung from the high ceilings, casting a warm, golden glow over the room. Marble columns were wrapped in lush garlands of white roses and ivy, and elegant tables were adorned with towering centerpieces of orchids and lilies. It must have cost at least two million dollars, and every penny was visible in the grandeur of the venue.

The opulence didn't stop at the chandeliers and floral arrangements or the hand selected food and drinks. He'd even had some vineyard in France make a special brand of nonalcoholic champagne so the underaged guests could toast with everyone else. Which was honestly wild. Everywhere I looked, there were signs of the extravagance that only Atticus could pull off.

Ice sculptures of mythical creatures, a live string quartet playing softly in one corner, and waiters circulating with trays of the finest hors d'oeuvres and champagne. The air was filled with the scent of the most expensive perfumes mingling together, and laughter echoed off the marble walls.

But even in the midst of all this splendor, I couldn't shake the feeling of longing that had settled deep in my chest. Seeing Gwen so deliriously happy with Atticus made me acutely aware of the emptiness I felt.

I tried to keep my smile bright, to join in the celebrations, but my eyes betrayed me, constantly seeking out Lance in the crowd.

He was always surrounded by people, his easy charm drawing them in. But every now and then, I caught him glancing my way, his expression thoughtful, almost worried. Did he see through my facade? Did he know how much I was struggling?

Gwen and Atticus were in the center of the dance floor, spinning around in their own little world. She looked radiant, and he couldn't take his eyes off her. Their happiness was infectious, spreading smiles all around.

I stood off to the side, nursing a glass of champagne, trying not to let my eyes follow Lance as he moved through the crowd. He looked dashing in his suit, laughing with Micah and some of the other guys. Every time I caught a glimpse of him, my heart did a little flip. But I couldn't let anyone see that. Not tonight.

"Hey, Morgan," Rowan said, appearing beside me with a friendly smile. "Care to dance?"

I hesitated for a moment, glancing over at Lance again before turning back to Rowan. "Sure, why not?"

Rowan led me to the dance floor, and we started to sway to the music. He was a good dancer, confident and smooth. "You look beautiful tonight," he said, his tone casual but sincere.

"Thanks, Rowan. You clean up pretty well yourself." And he did. He was handsome with a genuine sweet smile you couldn't help but respond to. Not to mention he was on the team of badasses my newly minted brother-in-law-again employed.

And he was closer to my age I thought. I'd heard Pierce call him the baby once.

So why didn't I feel anything but lukewarm affection when I looked at him.

Because my pussy was an asshole.

Pussy: No, that's the other guy.

I had to bite back my laugh as ee danced for a minute, lest he think I was insane. Just as I was starting to relax and enjoy myself when Lance stepped up, his expression unreadable, tapping Rowan on the shoulder. "Mind if I cut in?"

Rowan shrugged with a grin. "Not at all." He stepped back, and Lance took his place, his hand settling on my waist.

"Hi," he said, his voice low and familiar.

"Jackass," I replied, trying to keep my voice steady. "I was enjoying myself."

"Oh c'mon, we both know Rowan is a snooze fest. You'd much rather fight with me."

I immediately tried to twist out of his arms. Not because he was wrong, but because he was right. Just being in his vicinity, made my pulse race and my breathing shallow. "Can't you just go annoy someone else? My cousin Tara is right there. She looks bored and she needs a rebound, so bother her."

He pressed his lips firmly together, then surprised me and said, "How about, just for tonight, we call a truce."

I tried to let the tension roll off my shoulders. This was Gwen's second wedding. The least the two of us could do was try to get along for a dance. We danced in silence for a moment before Lance spoke again. I tried to let the tension roll off my shoulders. We danced in silence for a moment before Lance spoke again. "You okay? You look a bit... off."

I forced a smile. "I'm fine. It's just... watching Gwen and Atticus, they're so happy. I love seeing her like this."

Lance nodded, his eyes searching mine. "But?"

"But..." I sighed. "it's been just the two of us for so long. Now it's officially *not* just the two of us. It's a little sad."

His expression softened. "Hey, it's okay to feel like that. It's a big change."

I nodded, trying to blink away the tears that threatened

to fall. "I know. And I'm really happy for her, I am. It's just... different." I blinked rapidly to stop the impending waterworks. What was wrong with me? I was so damn happy for Gwen. And I loved Atticus for her.

The man was unhinged, but completely in love with my sister.

Lance released me and took my hand. "Come with me."

"Where are we going?" I asked as I followed him out onto the hidden balcony, the cool night air a welcome change from the warmth inside. The city lights stretched out before us, twinkling like the stars above. The skyline was breathtaking, a perfect backdrop for such a glamorous night.

"I figured you could use a moment."

Damn it. I hated it when he was sweet. It was harder to pretend when he was sweet. So much easier when he was his usual Lance self.

I placed my hands on the balcony stone railing and let the cool night air clear my head as I tipped my face up to the stars. Change was good. I just had to get over the loneliness.

When Lance spoke, his voices all gravel. "So are we never going to talk about it?"

I turned to meet his gaze. "Talk about what, Lance?"

He stood slo close but didn't touch me. The three inches between us suddenly the size of the Grand Canyon.

"This. The thing between us."

The bottom fell out of my stomach.

No. He was not doing this now. There was a delicate

balance between us. Mostly because, we never, ever, upon penalty of death spoke about that night. He was not bringing this shit up now.

When in doubt, deny, deny, deny. "I don't know what you're talking about."

I had to get out of here. When I turned to leave, he caught my wrist. His thumb stroked over the inside of my wrist. And I'm not going to lie, I almost folded. But I held my ground and lifted my chin defiantly.

That was until he leaned forward, and whispered, "You're a liar. Want me to prove it?"

Thank you so much for reading MERGER! Wow, what a ride! Gwen and Atticus finally getting a HEA. But I know you're thinking — BUT WHAT ABOUT MORGAN AND LANCE??? Find out what happens with our favorite enemies to lovers couple——>

FIND OUT IN DEEP POCKETS!

NANA MALONE READING LIST

Looking for a few Good Books? Look no Further

FREE

Cheeky Royal
The Heir
Bridge of Love

Mistletoe Series
Mistletoe Kisses
Mistletoe Hearts

Gentlemen Rogues
The Heir
The King
The Saint

Nana Malone Reading List

The Rook
The Spy
The Villain

Royals
Royals Undercover

Cheeky Royal
Cheeky King

Royals Undone
Royal Bastard
Bastard Prince

Royals United
Royal Tease
Teasing the Princess

Royal Elite

The Heiress Duet

Protecting the Heiress
Tempting the Heiress

The Prince Duet
Return of the Prince

Nana Malone Reading List

To Love a Prince

The Bodyguard Duet
Bodyguard to the Billionaire
The Billionaire's Secret

London Royals

London Royal Duet
London Royal
London Soul

Playboy Royal Duet
Royal Playboy
Playboy's Heart

London Lords
See No Evil
Big Ben
The Benefactor
For Her Benefit

Hear No Evil
East End
East Bound
Fall of East

Nana Malone Reading List

To Catch a Thief

Speak No Evil
Bridge of Love
London Bridge
Bridge of Lies
Broken Bridge

The Donovans Series
Come Home Again (Nate & Delilah)
Love Reality (Ryan & Mia)
Race For Love (Derek & Kisima)
Love in Plain Sight (Dylan and Serafina)
Eye of the Beholder – (Logan & Jezzie)
Love Struck (Zephyr & Malia)

London Billionaires Standalones
Mr. Trouble (Jarred & Kinsley)
Mr. Big (Zach & Emma)
Mr. Dirty (Nathan & Sophie)

The Player
Bryce
Dax
Echo
Fox
Ransom

Gage

The In Stilettos Series
Sexy in Stilettos (Alec & Jaya)
Sultry in Stilettos (Beckett & Ricca)
Sassy in Stilettos (Caleb & Micha)
Strollers & Stilettos (Alec & Jaya & Alexa)
Seductive in Stilettos (Shane & Tristia)
Stunning in Stilettos (Bryan & Kyra)
Tempting in Stilettos (Serena & Tyson)
Teasing in Stilettos (Cara & Tate)
Tantalizing in Stilettos (Jaggar & Griffin)

Love Match Series
*Game Set Match (Jason & Izzy)
Mismatch (Eli & Jessica)

Don't want to miss a single release? Click here!

Made in the USA
Monee, IL
22 August 2024